Welcome to Suite 4B!

Gone to the stables

Gina

Shh!! Studying—
please do not disturb!

Mary Beth

GO AWAY!!!

Andie

Hey, guys!
Meet me downstairs in the common room. Bring popcorn!

Lauren

Join Andie, Jina, Mary Beth, and Lauren for more fun at the Riding Academy!

#1 • *A Horse for Mary Beth*
#2 • *Andie Out of Control*
#3 • *Jina Rides to Win*
#4 • *Lessons for Lauren*

And coming soon:

#5 • *Mary Beth's Haunted Ride*
#6 • *Andie Shows Off*

"What's going on?" the stable manager demanded.

Lauren opened and shut her mouth like a fish. "Um," she stammered finally, "Ashley's fine. She was just tired from the show and tripped over—um—the bridle reins."

The stable manager pushed past Lauren and strode into the tack room. Lauren could hear Ashley's shrill voice protesting that everything was all right.

Half in a daze, Lauren went over to Whisper. Jina handed her the reins.

"Are *you* okay?" Jina asked.

"Really, Lauren. You look white as a ghost," Andie said.

Lauren shook her head. "I'm okay." But she wasn't. The doubts about Ashley were flooding back. Lauren wanted to tell her roommates what had really happened.

But she couldn't. She'd *promised*.

LESSONS FOR LAUREN

by Alison Hart

BULLSEYE BOOKS
Random House New York

A BULLSEYE BOOK PUBLISHED BY RANDOM HOUSE, INC.

 Published in the United States by Random House, Inc., New York, and simultaneously in Canada by Random House of Canada Limited, Toronto.

Library of Congress Catalog Card Number: 93-86086

ISBN: 0-679-85695-1

RL: 4.9

Manufactured in the United States of America

10 9 8 7 6 5 4 3 2 1

"Lauren! You're too stiff!" Katherine Parks, Foxhall Academy's dressage instructor, called from the middle of the ring.

Lauren Remick gritted her teeth. There were three other riders trotting a circle at the other end of the indoor ring. Why was Katherine always yelling at *her*?

Because you're the lousiest rider, Lauren told herself as her fingers tensed on the reins.

Immediately, Whisper raised her nose and pulled on the reins, trying to get away from Lauren's heavy grip. The chestnut horse's smooth trot grew choppy, and Lauren bumped in the saddle like a sack of potatoes.

"Lauren!" Katherine's voice was sharp. "Gentle those hands. If you're going to do well at the dressage competition, you're going to have to relax."

Lauren nodded. She didn't need to be reminded. The aim of dressage was to be a partner with your horse. That meant she had to work *with* Whisper—not against her.

As they trotted along the outside wall of the indoor ring, Lauren caught a glimpse of herself in the big wall mirror. She really *did* look like a wooden doll. And Whisper was sticking her nose up in the air, making her back hollow and her stride stiff.

No wonder Katherine was yelling at her.

Frustrated, Lauren slowed Whisper to a walk. Katherine waved for them to come into the middle of the ring.

Oh no, Lauren thought, *here it comes: the big lecture.*

Loosening her grip on the reins, she let Whisper stretch out her neck at the free walk. Then Lauren reluctantly looked over at Katherine.

The instructor was tapping a long dressage whip against her leg and frowning. Two years ago, Katherine Parks had taken over the dressage program at Foxhall Academy, a private boarding school for girls in Maryland. This year, Katherine hoped to have several riders good enough to win at local competitions.

"Lauren, what's going on?" Katherine's tone was matter-of-fact when Whisper halted next to her. "You're acting as though this is torture."

It *is* torture, Lauren felt like saying. Instead, she stared down at Whisper's chestnut mane and shook her head. "I don't know what's wrong."

The moment she said it, Lauren realized it wasn't true. She did know what was wrong. But it had to do with her schoolwork—not her riding.

"Well, okay. We all have bad days," Katherine said, smiling. Lauren thought the instructor was really pretty. She had glossy brown hair cut stylishly short, and almost always wore leather chaps and paddock boots since she was on and off horses all day.

"So, Ms. Remick, what can we do to get you to loosen up?" Katherine asked. "How about a few exercises?"

Lauren groaned. Every rider hated exercises. They were *real* torture.

Katherine put on her riding helmet and took Whisper's reins. "I'll ride Whisper around while I'm instructing the other girls. And you can do—let's see..." Putting a finger on her cheek, Katherine pretended to think. "Deep breathing, then fifty shoulder shrugs and rag doll rolls. *That* should loosen you up."

With a sigh, Lauren swung her right leg over Whisper's back and dropped lightly to the sawdust-and-sand-covered floor.

Katherine mounted Whisper and rode to the outside of the ring. Whisper moved easily in a balanced, light trot.

Lauren sighed. Katherine made everything look so easy. And dressage wasn't easy—there was so much to remember.

At the competition, she and Whisper would ride a solo test, performing a series of movements at the different gaits—walk, trot, and canter. A judge would award points on how well each movement was performed.

Lauren knew that Whisper hated it when she tensed up. Sitting in the saddle like a wooden doll would get them a big fat "one" on every movement. And out of ten points, a score of one meant "very bad."

Lauren sighed again as she began swiveling her head in endless circles. She had to admit, it served her right. Even if she was having problems with her schoolwork, she shouldn't let them affect her riding.

Not if she wanted to do well at the dressage competition in two weeks.

And she really, *really* wanted to do well.

"Can you believe Ms. Thaney?" Andie Perez grumbled from her bed in suite 4B that night. She was lying on her back, her stockinged feet stuck in the air, a notebook propped open on her chest. "That slave driver gave us *twenty* history questions!"

"So?" Mary Beth Finney countered. She was flopped on her stomach on her own bed, one hand propping up her chin as she read a science text. Her straight auburn hair fell like curtains against her cheeks. "I've finished them already."

"Finished!" Andie dropped her feet to the floor, her dark eyes snapping. "How could you be finished?"

"I'm done, too," Jina Williams said from the floor. Jina's tight black curls were pushed back by a red headband that matched her red plaid nightshirt. She was leaning against the side of her bed, reading *Lameness in Horses*. "That's because I worked for the last hour instead of complaining."

"Complaining!" Andie tossed her thick, wavy dark hair. "Who's complaining?"

Lauren stuck her fingers in her ears and hunched further over her desk. Andie was loud enough, but when all three of her roommates got to bickering, the noise bounced off the walls. The suite they shared had four desks, four dressers, and four beds squeezed into one tiny room, and things could get pretty tight. Especially during the two-hour evening study time when all Foxhall students had to stay in their suites.

Lauren stared at her open math text, trying to concentrate. Her class had been working on decimals. Dirty, dopey, dumb decimals.

Her teacher, Mrs. Jacquin, had explained everything patiently, but Lauren still didn't get it. That's why she was in the dummy math class. With a sigh of frustration, Lauren erased her last answer.

Andie fell back on her bed. "Well, I'll be finished with all my homework soon, too. You guys just wait."

I won't be finished, Lauren thought. *I'll be erasing all night.* Tiredly, she looped a few loose strands of honey blond hair behind her ears.

"Need help, Lauren?" Mary Beth asked from behind her.

Lauren spun around in the desk chair. Mary Beth was looking over her shoulder, her green eyes studying the math paper with all its mistakes.

"Decimals," Mary Beth said, nodding. "They're easy. I had them in fourth grade."

Embarrassed, Lauren quickly covered her paper with her hand. "Thanks, but I don't need any help," she said. "Like you said, they're a piece of cake."

"Okay." Mary Beth went over to her own desk and started putting her books away.

Lauren turned back to her math book. She'd answered ten problems, and she was sure they were wrong. Still, she didn't dare let Mary Beth help her. Her roommates already knew she was repeating sixth grade. If they found out she was still having trouble with math, they'd think she was *really* stupid.

Suddenly, Andie tossed her notebook in the air and jumped off the bed. "Nine o'clock! Study time's over!" She crossed the room in three bounds and yanked open the door.

Lauren could hear the buzz of voices as

girls streamed from their rooms. It sounded as if everybody in Bracken Hall were finished with their homework.

Everybody but her.

Jina threw her book on her quilt-covered bed and got up from the floor. "I'm going to call my mom."

"Come on, Lauren, let's get a soda," Mary Beth suggested. The sixth, seventh, and eighth graders had an hour to visit or go downstairs to the Common Room before lights-out.

"Sure." Lauren closed her math book. She needed a break.

The hall was crowded with girls. Everyone wore comfortable clothes—baggy sweats, jeans, slippers, robes, and pajamas. Andie was leaning against a doorjamb, chatting with the girls who lived next to them in suite 4C. Jina was using the pay phone down the hall.

"Are you okay?" Mary Beth asked Lauren as the two of them started down the steps to the first floor. "You've been so quiet the last few days. Are you mad at me about something?"

"I'm not mad at you," Lauren said quickly. "What makes you think that?"

Mary Beth shrugged. "Well, sometimes you act like I'm not even around lately. Like being with me is some kind of torture."

"That's what Katherine said about my riding," Lauren muttered as a group of chattering girls pushed past her.

"But I saw you ride today—you looked great!" Mary Beth said. "I watched you canter Whisper as Dan and I were plodding around the ring. You guys looked like something out of a Black Stallion movie." She peered at Lauren closely as they headed down the hall. "I know riding's not your problem."

Lauren bit her lip. She might as well face it. She couldn't hide the truth from Mary Beth.

"There is something wrong," Lauren said finally, stopping outside the Common Room.

"What? What's wrong?" Mary Beth prompted anxiously.

"I'm flunking math," Lauren blurted out.

There. She'd said it. Now Mary Beth would know what a total dummy she was.

"Flunking?" Mary Beth wrinkled her nose in disbelief. "You mean, like a D? Or worse?"

Lauren nodded. "Yeah. And that's not all," she said, her lower lip quivering. "If I can't pull my grade up by midterms, they'll kick me out of the riding program!"

Mary Beth's mouth fell open. "Kick you out of the riding program! But then you wouldn't be able to enter the dressage competition!"

"I know," Lauren said glumly.

She and Mary Beth turned into the Common Room. A dozen girls bustled around, fixing snacks, watching TV, playing games, and talking. "But you know Foxhall's policy," Lauren went on. "Academics come first."

"But I don't get it," Mary Beth said, her expression still puzzled. "Whenever I ask, you always say you don't need any help with math."

Lauren stopped in front of the soda machine and stuck three quarters in the slot. "That's because I don't want Andie teasing me," she said. "You're in the brainy math class, and Jina whizzes right through pre-algebra." She pulled out the soda, popped the top, and sighed. "And I'm in a special math class for girls who need help, and I'm still flunking."

"Wow." Mary Beth whistled softly.

For a few moments, the two girls silently sipped their drinks. Lauren leaned back against the soda machine, watching two other sixth-grade girls play Ping-Pong.

She bet *they* weren't flunking math.

"Well, I wish you'd told me before," Mary Beth said. "You've helped me lots with my riding. I could have helped you with math. Why don't I check tonight's homework?"

"Okay. Thanks." Lauren nodded, glad that she'd finally told somebody. "Only I think they're all wrong," she added, her gaze darting nervously to Mary Beth.

Her friend only grinned. "That's okay. I'll just have to show you how to make them all right!"

The next day in class, Mrs. Jacquin, the bubbly math teacher, handed Lauren her homework paper. "One hundred percent, Ms. Remick," she announced. "A super job."

Lauren grinned happily. It was the first A

she'd gotten all year. *I owe you one, Mary Beth,* she thought.

"Since you seem to understand the material so well, why don't you go up to the board and explain this decimal problem to the class?" Mrs. Jacquin continued.

Lauren's smile faded as the other girls in the class turned to look at her expectantly.

Last night, Mary Beth had made the problems look so easy. This morning, Lauren didn't have a clue how her roommate had solved them.

"Um," Lauren stammered, trying to figure out a way to get out of this. What would Andie do?

Suddenly, she clutched her stomach and leaned over the desk. "I think I'm going to be sick," she croaked. She jumped up so fast her chair almost fell over.

Mrs. Jacquin's eyes widened. "Please! Hurry to the rest room," she said, thrusting the wooden hall pass into Lauren's right hand.

Still doubled over, Lauren ran from the classroom and down the hall.

Quick thinking, Remick, she congratulated herself as she hurried down the hall. Her rolling stomach told her she wasn't bluffing.

She really was going to be sick!

When she reached the small bathroom at the end of the hall, she locked the door and quickly splashed cold water on her cheeks. Then she took deep breaths until the feeling of nausea slowly passed.

Looking up, she met her gaze in the mirror. Her face was chalky white. Her blue eyes were huge.

Someone rattled the doorknob. "Hey! You done in there yet?"

Lauren recognized Andie's voice. Just the person she *didn't* want to see. Quickly, she wiped her face with a paper towel, then smoothed back her hair with her fingers.

When she finally opened the bathroom door, Andie was standing outside with her arms crossed.

Andie snorted. "What were you *doing* in there? Giving yourself a makeover?"

"No." Lauren bit her lip. "I felt sick."

Andie squinted at her. "So what's wrong with you?"

"Breakfast was gross, that's all," Lauren said. Stepping around Andie, she marched down the hall.

When Lauren got back to class, Mrs.

Jacquin was leaning over Carrie's desk, explaining a problem. Lauren was sure everyone was staring at her as she slid into her own chair.

"Are you okay?" Sasha whispered.

Lauren nodded. "Yeah, I'm feeling a little better." She opened her textbook to the homework assignment written on the blackboard.

More division problems.

Her stomach lurched again.

Mrs. Jacquin came up beside her. "Is everything all right now?"

"I think so," Lauren whispered.

Luckily, the bell rang just then. Lauren shut her textbook and started to get up.

Mrs. Jacquin put a hand on her shoulder. "I'd like you to stay for a few minutes, Lauren. I need to speak with you."

Lauren froze halfway out of her seat. *This is it,* she thought. *Here's where she tells me I'm flunking.* She watched as the other girls left, whispering together and glancing over their shoulders.

They all know, Lauren thought.

When the room was quiet, Mrs. Jacquin came over and sat on the desk in front of Lauren's. She looked concerned.

With a sinking feeling, Lauren slumped in her chair.

"Lauren, I'm worried about you," the teacher said. "You work so hard in class. But on tests and homework, it's as though you've forgotten everything we went over."

Lauren's grip tightened on her books. She couldn't look at her teacher. "I know. My grades aren't so good, are they?"

Mrs. Jacquin sighed. "No, they're not. Even with a B for effort and classroom participation."

Lauren swallowed hard. She'd had the same conversation last year at her old school.

"Lauren, you're in this particular class because you need help in math," the teacher went on. "But I don't seem to be reaching you."

"Oh, but you are!" Lauren protested. "When I'm here in the class, the math makes sense. But later, when I sit down to do my homework, I forget everything. The same goes with tests. I think I know everything, but the day of the test, my mind goes blank."

"Hmmmm." Mrs. Jacquin looked thoughtful. "That gives me an idea. What if you had some tutoring sessions after school? Someone to help you with your homework and prepare you for tests."

"A tutor?"

Mrs. Jacquin nodded. "An upper-school student who could explain things when you got stuck."

"That might work," Lauren said slowly. "My roommate Mary Beth helped me with last night's homework." She blushed. "That's why I did so well on it."

"Well, I couldn't assign another sixth-grader, but let me talk to Mr. Lyons, your counselor," Mrs. Jacquin said. "We'll see if the two of us can't come up with someone. How does that sound?"

Lauren grinned. "Great." Suddenly, she felt one hundred percent better.

Mrs. Jacquin smiled, too. "There are only two weeks left before midterms. Let's see if we can pull your grade up before then."

Two weeks! Lauren's heart dropped. In order to stay in the riding program, she'd have to pull her grade up to at least a C plus.

The student picked to be her tutor would have to perform a miracle!

"Remember, Lauren. The walk may seem easy, but it's an important gait," Katherine said as Lauren and Whisper circled around her. "In the competition a week from Saturday, you'll have to demonstrate a working walk."

Lauren nodded. She was riding Whisper in the outdoor dressage arena. The arena was a large rectangle surrounded by a low white fence. Bold black letters written on three-sided markers were mounted right outside the fence. The markers guided horse and rider through their movements.

"Keep light contact on the reins," Katherine continued, "but close your legs tighter around Whisper's sides. That will tell her to reach with her hind legs."

Lauren sighed. She had been tightening her

legs until her calves ached. It was hard to get a horse to walk correctly. And Whisper liked to dawdle along and look at the other horses.

"We'll pretend we're taking a dressage test," Katherine continued. "I want you to ride from *A* to *P* at a working walk." Katherine waved at the markers outside the arena. "Next, do a free walk from *P* to *S*, then pull her together again for a working walk from *S* to *C*."

That sounded easy, but Lauren knew from her training level tests last summer that the judges really scored tough when it came to the walk. If she was going to keep from losing points, she'd have to make this movement strong.

"Okay, Whisper," she murmured, "let's do it, girl."

When they reached marker *A*—the entrance to the arena—Lauren deepened her seat and closed her legs on Whisper's sides. At the same time she increased Whisper's contact with the bit. Whisper flicked her ears back, then pricked them forward again. The mare arched her neck and her pace quickened.

Too quick, Lauren thought. The judge didn't want to see short, hurried steps. Instantly,

Lauren did a half-halt, closing her fingers and legs to ask for a longer stride.

"Terrific!" Katherine shouted.

Lauren grinned. It *had* felt great. Whisper moved forward smoothly. It was like riding a cloud.

As she approached the *P* marker, Lauren pressed her inside leg against the girth. At the same time, she slid her outside leg behind the girth to bend Whisper as they turned to cross the arena diagonally. Then she loosened her reins for the free walk, hoping Whisper wouldn't break into a jig. The mare stretched out her neck and took long easy strides as she crossed the arena diagonally to *S*.

Loud clapping made Lauren glance up. Alicia, Nicole, and Ginny, the other dressage riders, were applauding her.

Lauren thought she'd die from happiness.

Half an hour later, she bathed Whisper in the grass-covered courtyard in front of Foxhall's main barn. The barn was shaped like a horseshoe so that the twenty stalls faced the courtyard. Katherine Parks's office and the tack room were located at the right end of the building.

Lauren sponged warm water on Whisper's back and belly. The mare lifted her lip in the air and wiggled it with pleasure.

"You silly thing." Lauren laughed as she scratched the mare's itchy stomach. Then she scraped off the excess water with a sweat scraper.

Even though the October air was crisp, the chestnut mare had worked up a lather. Lauren needed to get her cool and dry before putting her back in her stall for the night.

Jina walked toward them across the courtyard, leading Superstar, her handsome gray Thoroughbred. Bright red wraps encased his lower legs.

"How'd it go today?" Jina asked.

"Great!" Lauren told her. "Whisper was smooth as a milkshake."

Jina laughed, and Superstar halted and stretched out his neck to sniff Whisper. The mare pawed the ground with one hoof and squealed.

"Hey!" Jina jerked on Superstar's lead line. "He's been so full of himself these last few days," she explained. "I'll be glad when I don't have to walk him anymore."

During the last horse show, Superstar had

bowed a tendon in his front leg. The vet had said it was only a slight bow, but Jina wouldn't be able to ride him or even turn him out in the pasture for weeks. That meant she had to hand walk him in the afternoons.

"If Dorothy didn't take him out in the morning while I'm at classes, he'd be a real brat," Jina added as Superstar snorted and pranced sideways.

Just then, another horse and rider came toward them across the courtyard.

"Uh-oh, don't look now," Lauren whispered. "It's Ashley Stewart."

Jina's eyes narrowed. "The last person I want to see," she muttered between clenched teeth.

"Jina!" Ashley called. She was mounted on a sleek chestnut mare named April Fool. Ashley, a popular junior, was slim and petite and had a natural seat on a horse. Lauren envied the older girl's fashionable houndstooth riding leggings and matching waist-length jacket.

"Superstar looks fat and sassy," Ashley said when she halted April. "Too bad he won't be competing anymore this year."

Lauren glanced at Jina. Her roommate was fiddling with Superstar's mane, trying to ignore

Ashley. The older girl had been Jina's rival at many of the shows, and she hadn't hidden her anger when Jina had beaten her out.

Lifting his head high, Superstar whinnied at April. Then he lunged forward, nearly pulling the lead strap from Jina's grasp.

"Whoa," Jina said, yanking on the halter.

"I guess I have a good chance at the Junior Horse of the Year Award," Ashley continued smugly. "Though I probably would have won it anyway."

Lauren's mouth fell open. Ashley was such a good rider and April was such a good horse, the pair probably *would* have won. Ashley didn't have to rub it in, though.

"Why don't you lighten up, Ashley?" Lauren said sharply. "Jina feels bad enough."

"Sorry," Ashley said, shrugging. "By the way, Lauren, I hear you and I are going to be spending lots of time together."

"What do you mean?" Lauren asked. Beside her, Whisper tugged on the lead, trying to get her head down for a bite of grass.

"I guess you haven't talked to Mr. Lyons yet."

Lauren frowned, puzzled. "Mr. Lyons? My counselor?"

"Yeah. He's my counselor, too. And he mentioned you need help with math."

Lauren gulped. Why would he tell Ashley that? She glanced over at Jina, wondering if her roommate was listening. But Jina was letting Superstar graze about five feet away.

"He said Mrs. Jacquin thought you needed a tutor," Ashley explained. "And I just happen to need a project for my junior service credit."

Oh no. Lauren gripped the lead line tightly, afraid of what Ashley was about to say.

"So it looks like *I'm* going to be your math tutor, Lauren," Ashley said, grinning broadly. "What do you think about that?"

I think it stinks, Lauren thought as she stared at the older girl. Ashley "the Snob" Stewart was her new tutor?

"*You're* going to help Lauren with math?" Jina asked Ashley as she led Superstar closer. She sounded as shocked as Lauren felt.

"Yeah. Isn't that great?" Still grinning, Ashley looked back and forth at the two girls. "So you'd better be nice to me, Lauren. And hey, Jina, I *am* sorry Superstar bowed. Really," she added. Then, turning April, she rode past them toward the riding ring.

Jina wrinkled her nose in distaste as she watched Ashley ride off. Then she turned to Lauren. "So what do you need a tutor for? I didn't know you were still having trouble with math. Aren't you in a special math class?"

Lauren nudged the grass with the toe of her riding boot. "Yeah, I am," she muttered. Whisper pushed her with her nose, and Lauren stumbled forward. "Well, I'd better put a sweat sheet on Whisper and finish cooling her off."

"I'll come with you," Jina offered. "It's nice to have company while I walk Superstar."

The two girls started toward Whisper's stall, their horses walking beside them. Jina didn't say anything, but Lauren knew what her roommate was thinking. Jina had only gotten one C in her entire life. She had no idea what it was like to flunk a class.

"So tell me about this pony you're going to show," Lauren said, hoping to change the subject.

Jina shrugged. "His name's Applejacks. I haven't met him yet, but I've heard lots about him from Whitney Chambers."

"She's the little girl who owns him, right?"

Jina stopped walking. "I wish I'd known you were having a hard time, Lauren. I would have helped."

Lauren kept her eyes on the ground. "There wasn't anything you could do." She halted Whisper in front of the stall where she'd draped the sweat sheet over the door.

"I could have done *something*," Jina insisted.

"Maybe." Lauren shrugged as she covered Whisper's damp back with the lightweight sheet. "But you had enough stuff to worry about—showing, Superstar's injury, and trying not to let Ashley get to you."

"Yeah. She can be a jerk." Jina glanced sideways at Lauren. "And just think—she's going to be your tutor!"

"I can't believe you're stuck with snotty Ashley," Andie said to Lauren that evening during study time. Dressed in raggedy leggings, a baggy flannel shirt, and wool socks, she was sitting on her bed, cracking peanuts. Pieces of shell flew on the floor.

"Believe it," Lauren replied as she stuck her math notebook in her backpack. "And my first tutoring session is tonight."

"What's she going to teach you?" Andie continued, stuffing a peanut in her mouth. "How to be a snob in three days or less?"

Lauren reached for her hooded sweatshirt. "Hopefully, she's going to teach me how to divide decimals."

Mary Beth looked up from her desk next to

Lauren's. She was dressed in sweatpants, her bangs pulled back with hair clips. Pimple cream dotted her forehead. "Ashley is in the advanced junior math class," she pointed out. "So she must know her stuff."

Lauren zipped up the sweatshirt. "All I want her to know is decimals."

Andie snorted. "I know decimals. Why didn't they assign me to be your tutor?"

"They probably figured you'd teach her how to cheat," Mary Beth taunted.

"Hey!" Andie threw a peanut at her. Laughing, Mary Beth threw it right back.

Lauren slung her pack over her shoulder and glanced at Jina. She was sprawled on her bed, ignoring her roommates.

"Are you going to help me keep these two from killing each other?" Lauren asked.

"No," Jina said flatly. "Let them. Then there will be more closet space for us."

Lauren laughed. "See you guys later."

"If *I* had permission to leave the dorm during study time, I'd make a break for it," Andie called as Lauren opened the door of the suite.

Lauren shut the door behind her, cutting Andie off. The hall was dead quiet. That afternoon, she'd received permission to go over to Mill Hall, Ashley's dorm, every school night for forty-five minutes.

When she got outside, Lauren jogged down the walk, the brisk wind tugging her hair from its braid. The campus was dark, and the overhead lights created eerie shadows.

Finally, she reached Mill Hall, a three-story brick building at the end of the grassy courtyard. Many of the older girls chose the newer dorm because the suites and bathrooms were larger. Lauren was glad her sister, Stephanie, a junior like Ashley, had stayed in Bracken Hall. When Lauren felt homesick it helped to have her sister close by.

Ashley roomed in suite 2C, but they were supposed to meet downstairs to study in Mill Hall's Common Room.

"Hi, Lauren," Ashley greeted her cheerfully when Lauren stepped into the large room. The older girl was sitting on a comfortable-looking sofa. She wore a long blue cashmere turtleneck over black velvet leggings.

"Hi." Lauren stopped in the doorway. Like the common area in Bracken Hall, this room had two groupings of sofas, a gleaming kitchenette, pool and Ping-Pong tables, two TVs with VCRs, a CD player, and a fireplace. Right now it was quiet since all the other students were studying in their suites.

"This is nice," she said, glancing hesitantly at Ashley. The older girl had always been so snotty to Lauren and her roommates, especially Jina. She had no idea how this whole tutoring idea was going to work out.

Ashley patted the seat next to her, then plopped her stockinged feet on the coffee table.

"Let's get to work. I want to finish by nine, so I can call my boyfriend then."

"Your boyfriend?" Lauren asked as she went over to the sofa. "Where does he live?"

"Steve goes to Manchester Academy. You know, that big deal boys' school near Baltimore."

"Hey, don't those guys come to Foxhall every year for the Halloween weekend?" Lauren sat down eagerly. She loved hearing stuff about guys.

Ashley grinned. "Yeah. That's when I met him, at last year's dance. I haven't seen him since school started."

"Are you going steady?" Lauren asked shyly.

Ashley nodded. Then she put a finger to her

lips. "Don't tell anyone," she whispered.

Lauren crossed her heart. "I promise. I won't tell a soul!" Slowly, she unzipped her backpack. It was so neat to have an older girl like Ashley confide in her, a lowly sixth-grader.

"I bet you have a boyfriend, too," Ashley said.

Lauren busied herself with pulling her math books from her pack. "Not really. I just think this one guy's really cute."

Ashley leaned forward. "Who?"

"Todd Jenkins, Jina's train—" Flushing, Lauren caught herself. Ashley wouldn't want to hear anything about Jina.

"I've seen him at the shows," Ashley said, with a wave of her hand. "He is cute. And he's a good trainer, too. He's even given me a few riding tips." She leaned forward. "You know, I really don't care about Jina. I gave her a hard time at the shows sometimes—you know, to psych her out a little. She has to learn to keep her cool. That's what winning's all about."

"Oh," Lauren said, sitting down. "Well, about Todd. He's not my boyfriend or anything. I mean, he's too old for me."

Ashley smiled. "A crush on an older guy is fun. I've had lots of them."

"Really?" Lauren sat up straighter.

Ashley smiled coyly. "In fact, I've got one right now."

"No!" Lauren gasped. "Who?"

"Mr. Lyons."

"Mr. Lyons! Our counselor? But he's married."

Ashley laughed. "It's just a crush."

Lauren nodded, feeling stupid. "Right." For a moment, she studied Ashley, wondering why she was suddenly being so nice. The older girl's blond hair had been brushed into a sleek pageboy. Lauren touched her own braid. Maybe if she cut her hair, it would look as cute as Ashley's.

"So what's this about decimals?" Ashley asked, pointing to the unopened book on Lauren's lap.

"Oh, right." Quickly Lauren flipped to page 32. Her class had been assigned twenty division problems. "I understand them when Mrs. Jacquin explains them. But later..." Her voice trailed away.

Ashley nodded. "Oh, I know that feeling."

"You do?" Lauren was surprised. She'd thought Ashley always did everything right. "But aren't you in the highest math class?"

"Well, yeah. It's history stuff that drives me nuts. I memorize all those stupid facts before a test. Then the next day, poof!—they disappear."

"Wow." Lauren slumped back against the sofa cushions. Ashley was studying the page in the text.

"Okay, get out your notebook," Ashley said, her voice suddenly businesslike. "I'll show you a way to remember these division steps." She grinned at Lauren.

Lauren grinned back. How could she ever have thought Ashley was a snob? She'd been totally wrong!

"Ashley and I figured out all the steps needed to solve a division problem," Lauren told Mary Beth two days later, as they stood in the hot-food line at lunch. "After that, we made up a name for each step to help me remember them. It's called 'mnemonics.' Isn't that cool?"

"Cool," Mary Beth repeated, her attention on the food the cooks were slopping onto her plate. "But I don't have the foggiest idea what you're talking about."

Lauren gave her roommate an exasperated look, but she didn't reply. The cook was waiting for her order. "Steak sub with cheese, onions, and mushrooms—but no steak," she told him.

"No steak?" Mary Beth said. "You are so weird, Lauren."

"Well, did you look at it?" She pointed to the display tray behind the glass partition. "The steak has *pimples.*"

Mary Beth rolled her eyes. "So I'll squeeze zit cream on my sandwich."

Giggling, Lauren took her plate. As she followed Mary Beth over to the condiment table, she tried to explain how Ashley had made division seem easier. "She said the steps for division are divide, multiply, subtract, remainder, and bring down—"

"Bring down?" Mary Beth looked puzzled. "Is that a math term?"

"No! That's why it's so easy for me to remember!" Lauren exclaimed. She leaned across the table and, using a fork, speared several tomatoes to put on her sub.

"The second step is multiply," she continued, waving the fork at Mary Beth. "So we called that step—'Mary.' Get it? *M* for multiply and Mary. Mary's part of your name—so I'll always remember it."

"I'm flattered." Mary Beth squeezed a ton of ketchup on her sub. "But I still don't get it. Hey, Jina and Andie are waving to us."

Picking up her tray, Mary Beth headed toward a round table in the corner of the large cafeteria. Lauren followed her, weaving around the chairs filled with teachers and students. At dinner, the girls had assigned seats. But for breakfast and lunch, they could eat anywhere they wanted.

"Sit yourselves down," Andie called as the girls drew closer.

Next to her, Jina grimaced. "Andie," she hissed, "why do you always talk with your mouth full?"

Lauren set her tray next to Jina's.

"So how's snobby Ashley?" Andie asked, taking another bite of her tuna salad sub. Her wild hair was pulled back with a Scrunchie, so for once it didn't flop in her plate.

"She's not a snob, she's nice," Lauren defended her new tutor as she sat down.

"*Nice?*" Jina's fork froze in the air.

"Oops." Lauren clapped her hand to her mouth. "Sorry, Jina. I know she's been mean to you and all, but the last two nights she's really been a big help with my homework."

Andie and Jina exchanged glances, then looked over at Mary Beth.

"Has Remick flipped?" Andie asked Mary Beth.

Mary Beth shrugged. "I think so. She was

babbling about all sorts of strange stuff."

Lauren slammed her glass of juice on the table. "I should have known you guys wouldn't understand. You're *so-o-o* immature. Like about Todd and me. Now you won't even give poor Ashley a second chance."

"Immature?" Andie repeated in a huffy voice. "Look who's talking, Ms. Flat Chest."

"I am *not* flat," Lauren retorted, even though it was true. Jina snickered and Mary Beth broke into a fit of giggles. Grabbing her tray, Lauren whirled around and spotted Stephanie at another table. She'd go eat with her sister. In fact, she decided, she wouldn't eat with her roommates ever again!

"Lauren?" Mary Beth's voice came from outside Whisper's stall. It was late that afternoon, and Lauren was getting ready for her riding lesson.

Lauren ignored her and kept brushing Whisper. Harder and harder she stroked, until the mare angrily flattened her ears.

Mary Beth stepped into the stall doorway, a halter clasped in one hand. "I'm sorry for being such a jerk at lunch. You were trying to explain something, and I guess I wasn't being the best friend in the world."

Lauren stopped brushing. "No, you sure weren't. But I should have realized that Jina wouldn't want to hear how wonderful Ashley is."

She finally turned to look at her roommate. Mary Beth was scuffing her boots in the straw.

"Still friends?" Lauren asked.

Mary Beth grinned. "Still friends." She hesitated. "Uh, maybe you should be careful, though," she added.

"Careful?" Lauren dropped her brush in Whisper's grooming box and pulled out the hoof pick. "What are you talking about?"

Mary Beth bit her lip. "Well—you don't know Ashley that well, yet. You're forgetting how nasty she was to Jina."

"I haven't forgotten," Lauren protested.

"Okay, okay," Mary Beth said quickly, holding up her hands. Then she asked, "Are you and Whisper doing anything terrific in dressage class today?"

Lauren stepped back to look at the chestnut mare. Her coat gleamed, and Lauren had pulled her mane a little each day, thinning out the thick hair, so it finally lay flat on her neck. Whisper looked perfect. "I don't know about me," Lauren said, patting the mare's glossy neck, "but Whisper does something terrific every day!"

"Congrats, Lauren!" Ashley said in a pleased voice that night. She had been watching Lauren solve her last homework problem. "You did it! I only had to help you in two places."

Lauren beamed. She really *had* done it! She'd remembered every step, thanks to Ashley's tutoring.

The older girl pulled a calculator from under a pile of papers. She was sitting cross-legged on the sofa, a diet soda in her hand. "Now, here's the next thing you're going to do," she said.

Lauren's eyes widened. "But we're not allowed to use calculators."

"Sure you are." Ashley turned it on. "Not to solve the problems—to check them. Otherwise, how do you know whether you've done them right?"

"I never thought of that." Lauren took the calculator and punched in the first problem.

Ashley pointed to the answer. "See? The answer is a decimal, just like your problem. And you got it right!"

"Wow. I did," Lauren said in a surprised voice.

Ashley laughed. "You're acting like you never got a problem correct in your life." Yawning, she stood up and stretched. Her floppy sweater rode up over her ribs. Lauren could count every one.

Ashley's really skinny, Lauren thought, startled. She'd never noticed *how* skinny.

"Diet soda?" Ashley asked, heading toward the kitchenette.

Lauren quickly looked back at her homework paper. She didn't want Ashley to think she'd been staring at her. "No. I had a huge dinner. I couldn't fit in another thing."

Ashley made a face. "That stuff the cafeteria serves is so gross."

"You said it," Lauren agreed. "The only one who likes it is my roommate Mary Beth."

Ashley quickly did three deep knee bends and a few toe touches.

Lauren watched her. "What are you doing?"

Ashley started rotating her upper body. "My roommate, Penny, and I do an exercise video every night. You know, to keep in shape. You ought to try it."

Lauren shuddered. "No thanks."

"It's hard work, but it's fun. I feel great when I'm done, and it's good for my riding." She stopped rotating. "Penny and I lift weights at the gym, too. My muscles are getting like steel."

"Mmmm." Lauren punched the next set of numbers into the calculator, as Ashley continued to exercise. So far, most of her homework problems were right.

"Finished!" she declared triumphantly ten minutes later.

Ashley flopped down next to her, panting. "Let's see." She glanced over the paper. "Super. And you did it all yourself!"

"With your help." Lauren grinned shyly.

Ashley chucked her under the chin. "Right. Now come on, how about doing that exercise video with me?" She jumped up.

"But you just exercised for the last fifteen minutes," Lauren pointed out.

"Well, you can never be too fit," Ashley said. "After all, a judge doesn't want to see some chubbo bouncing up and down in the show ring. I still have to lose a few more pounds."

Lauren's eyes widened. "But you're thin enough already!"

"No way. My thighs are too fat. And now that Jina's out of the show circuit, I've got an even better chance to win that zone award. I don't want to blow everything because I look huge in my breeches."

Ashley looked pointedly at Lauren's stomach. Lauren dropped her chin to see what Ashley was staring at. Because she was sitting down, her jeans were bunched up a bit in front.

"Don't you want to look really great for your big dressage competition?" Ashley asked.

Lauren gulped. "Well, yeah, I guess so."

"Then you'd better work on flattening that stomach." Lauren frowned down at her lap. Immediately, she sucked in her stomach, trying to make it look flatter. Her zipper still bulged out.

"Gee, maybe you're right," Lauren murmured.

Ashley grinned. "Salads and exercise. *That*'ll get you a blue ribbon at that dressage show."

"Well, I'd sure love a blue ribbon." Lauren pressed her fingers against her stomach. Was she really getting fat? She'd never even noticed. "Maybe I'll do that exercise video with you after all!"

"One, two. Two, two," Lauren recited as she did sit-ups on her bed. It was seven o'clock in the morning. Andie and Jina were still huddled under their covers. Mary Beth had jumped into the shower. "Three, two. Four, two."

"*What* are you doing?" Andie peeked from under her blanket. "Some kind of weird math homework?"

"Exercises," Lauren puffed. "Five, two. Six, two."

"Don't you have any *quiet* exercises?" Andie grumbled.

Lauren stuck her tongue out, then kept counting. "Seven, two. Eight, two."

Yawning, Jina sat up in bed. "Why are you working out so much?" she asked, her golden eyes still sleepy.

"Ashley says my stomach's too fat," Lauren gasped between sit-ups.

Andie snorted as she flipped off the covers. "The only thing that's fat is Ashley's head."

Jina yawned again and stretched her arms high over her head. "I hope you don't want to look as skinny as her."

"She's not skinny, she's *fit*," Lauren said, flopping back and taking a few deep breaths. All those sit-ups had worn her out. Maybe she *wasn't* in such hot shape. "She does this exercise video twice every night with her roommate."

The bathroom door opened and a cloud of steam poured into the room.

"Next," Mary Beth sang out. She wore boxer shorts and a turtleneck. Her auburn bangs were plastered on her damp forehead.

Andie sprang out of bed and snatched up her bath bucket. "That's me," she said, disappearing into the bathroom.

Lauren dropped onto the bedroom floor and started doing push-ups.

Mary Beth stopped rummaging in her dresser drawer to look down at her. "What in the world are you doing?"

"Ex-er-ci-ses," Lauren puffed. "I keep telling

everyone I have to exercise."

"Don't ask her why," Jina put in. "It's something about being too fat."

"Too fat?" Mary Beth stared at Lauren. "No way."

With a gasp, Lauren flopped facedown onto the linoleum. "Ten!" she cried. Quickly, she checked her watch. "Uh-oh, I'd better hurry. I'm meeting Ashley for a run around the courtyard."

Mary Beth raised one brow. "Are you kidding? What about breakfast?"

"I'm going to skip it," Lauren said as she stood up and hurriedly tucked her knit shirt into her tan corduroys. She glanced down to check out her stomach. It definitely looked flatter.

"Are you crazy?" Mary Beth said. "They have fresh doughnuts Friday mornings."

"Doughnuts!" Lauren made a face. Then, picking up her windbreaker, she wagged a scolding finger at Mary Beth. "I wouldn't eat them if I were you. Ashley says they're practically poison!"

Later that morning, Lauren clapped her hand to her stomach, trying to keep it from growling. Without raising her head, she glanced around the classroom. Mrs. Jacquin was working at the blackboard with Sasha, Rene, and Carrie. Amy, the girl at the desk beside Lauren, was hunched over the paper on her desk, erasing furiously. No one had heard Lauren's stomach.

Lauren sighed and went back to her own paper. She could hardly wait till lunch next period. She was going to eat twelve sandwiches. Skipping breakfast had been so stupid. She didn't know how Ashley did it every single morning.

Mrs. Jacquin finished with the girls at the blackboard and came over to Lauren. Quickly, the teacher skimmed her paper.

"Nice job, Lauren. Next week, we'll review for the midterm. If you keep up the good work, you should do really well."

Thanks to Ashley, Lauren added to herself as the teacher walked away.

When the bell rang ten minutes later, Lauren quickly stuffed her books in her backpack. She had to hurry to meet Mary Beth in front of Eaton Hall.

She walked out of the math and science building with Carrie, Amy, and Sasha. The three girls were discussing their weekend plans.

"Saturday, my roommate and I are going to the mall," Carrie said. She was tall with shiny long brown hair that she always wore pulled back in a hair band. "The Foxhall van leaves after lunch. Anybody want to go with us?"

Sasha shook her head as they walked across the courtyard to Eaton Hall. "I've got field hockey intramurals."

"I'll go," Amy chimed in. Amy was short, with frizzy red hair. "But only if we'll be back in time for the Saturday night program. They're showing *International Velvet*."

"Is that the movie with Elizabeth Taylor?" Sasha asked. "I've already seen it a gazillion times."

"No, silly," Amy told her. "This is a newer one. With Tatum O'Neal."

Just then, Lauren spotted Mary Beth jogging across the courtyard. Her roommate had a huge grin on her face.

"I'll see you later, guys," Lauren told the others.

"Hi, Lauren!" Mary Beth called as she leaped up the steps of Eaton Hall. She had a package under one arm, an open letter in her hand, and a huge grin on her face.

"What are you so happy about?" Lauren asked.

Mary Beth held up the white envelope. "*This!* It's a letter from Brad, this guy I know back home."

Lauren's mouth fell open. "You got a letter from a *boy*?"

Mary Beth nodded excitedly. "Yup. I mean, it wasn't romantic or anything. He just talked about what all the kids back at Cedarville Elementary are up to, but..." She grinned as her voice trailed off.

"That's so cool." Lauren squeezed Mary Beth's wrist. "You're the first one in suite 4B to have a real live boyfriend this year."

Mary Beth blushed bright red. "Well, I don't know about the boyfriend part. But look what else I got!" She held out the package. "Mom sent more chocolate chip cookies."

"Cookies!" Lauren licked her lips. Mary Beth's mom made the world's best cookies, and she always sent a lot of them. "Hurry and open them!" Lauren said hungrily. Her stomach had already started growling again.

Sitting down on the steps, Mary Beth tore eagerly into the box. Lauren dropped her backpack and sat next to her roommate.

"Hey, guys, what's in the package?" Andie said. She was standing on the top step, looking down at them.

"Cookies!" Lauren and Mary Beth chorused.

"From Finney's mom?" Andie asked.

Still staring at the package, Lauren nodded. Mary Beth had ripped off all the brown paper. Underneath was a shoe box. Mary Beth lifted off the top, and peeled back the aluminum foil that covered the cookies.

Lauren's mouth watered. The cookies were beautiful golden circles of chips and nuts. She took a deep breath, inhaling the scent of chocolate, brown sugar, and butter.

Mary Beth held out the box. "You'd better take one, Lauren, before you keel over with excitement."

Andie bent down and grabbed a handful of cookies. "What's your problem, anyway, Remick?"

"Hungry," Lauren murmured, her teeth sinking into a cookie. It was crunchy on the outside, gooey on the inside. "Mmm. This is perfect."

Suddenly, there was a loud gasp behind

them. Lauren jerked her head around. Ashley had just come out of Eaton Hall. Her eyes were wide with disbelief as she stared at the girls.

"Lauren Remick!" she snapped. "*What* are you eating?"

Lauren stopped chewing. "A cookie," she replied hesitantly.

"A cookie!" Ashley exclaimed. "Don't you remember what we talked about? Salads and exercise! That's what will get you that blue ribbon."

Slowly, Lauren drew the cookie away from her mouth. Andie and Mary Beth were staring at Ashley as if she were crazy.

Was Ashley crazy? Lauren wondered. The older girl didn't look so hot today. She was dressed in a bulky knit sweater layered over a turtleneck. Her cheeks were sucked in and her lips were pinched together in anger.

No, Ashley wasn't crazy, Lauren decided, quickly pushing the thought out of her mind. She was confident and smart and cool. Still, she was definitely acting strangely.

Something was wrong with Ashley.

But Lauren had no idea what it was.

"Mary Beth's mom sent the cookies," Lauren told Ashley. "They're great. Try one."

Ashley made a disgusted face. "No way." Her lips turned down in a pout. "But if *you* want to eat them, go ahead. Just remember"—she stuck her finger in Lauren's face—"for every cookie you eat, that's at least half an hour of exercise."

Lauren nodded quickly. Spinning around, Ashley went down the steps.

"What's wrong with *her*?" Mary Beth asked when Ashley was out of sight.

Lauren shrugged. She wasn't sure herself. "Ashley's really into being healthy."

"She's into being weird if you ask me." Andie snorted as she stuffed a third cookie in her mouth. Mary Beth reached into the box and handed Lauren another cookie.

Lauren shook her head. "Ashley's right. I'd better not."

Andie stopped chewing. "Oh no. Don't tell me you're turning into an Ashley clone. One is bad enough."

Lauren hoisted her backpack over her shoulder and stood up, ignoring Andie. Her roommate just didn't know Ashley the way she did. "Ready for lunch, guys?"

"Sure." Mary Beth put the top back on the box.

"I heard they're having burgers and fries today."

"No fattening food for me," Lauren said with a sigh. That dressage competition was getting closer and closer.

"Hey, Jina, how about a trail ride tomorrow?" Lauren called as she led Whisper down the aisle of the new barn. She wore her helmet, tall black boots, and a Foxhall sweatshirt over an old pair of breeches. "Mrs. Caufield has a sign-up sheet for girls not going to the show."

Jina was kneeling beside Superstar, who stood patiently in crossties. "I don't have a horse to ride," she replied without looking up from Superstar's front leg. Dirty leg wraps were strewn on the concrete floor.

"That's okay." Lauren halted Whisper. "Mrs. Caufield said you and Andie can ride school horses. Not that many girls are going to the show, so Dorothy's staying behind to lead the trail ride."

Picking up a clean, rolled wrap, Jina started unwinding it around Superstar's front leg. "Oh, I don't know—"

"Jina," Lauren said impatiently, "you have to start riding again sometime. You don't have to quit totally just because Superstar's lame."

Jina sighed. "I know, I know. That's what Todd keeps telling me."

Lauren brightened. "How is Todd? I haven't seen him in ages."

"Still incredibly handsome," Jina teased. Then she grew serious again. "It just wouldn't be the same," she said slowly, "riding a horse other than Superstar."

"I understand," Lauren said. "But Saturday would just be a plain old fun trail ride."

Jina didn't answer. She secured the wrap with the Velcro tabs, then sat back on her heels to survey her work. The top of the wrap was already starting to sag.

Jina shook her head. "When Dorothy bandages a leg, it looks so professional."

"Yours is okay," Lauren told her. Then Superstar tossed his head impatiently and pawed the concrete floor with his hoof. The Velcro came loose with a loud rip.

Startled, Whisper threw up her head.

Jina rolled her eyes, then started laughing. "I guess I have to start all over again."

"So how about that trail ride?" Lauren pressed. "You need something to take your mind off Superstar."

"Well—" Jina hesitated, then she smiled slightly. "I guess you're right. I haven't been on a trail ride in ages. It might be fun."

"Good." Lauren waved good-bye, then headed to the outdoor ring with Whisper for their lesson.

A few minutes later, Lauren and Whisper were walking along the rail with the other dressage riders. The group had just warmed up by trotting large circles on a relaxed rein. Katherine stood in the middle of the ring, explaining the next part of the lesson.

"Okay, gang. Halts. For next Saturday's test, you will have two halts from a trot, then a salute. Your horse has to stand quietly with all four feet squarely underneath him while you wait for the judge to salute back. Sound easy?"

Lauren shook her head quickly. Last summer she'd forgotten to salute before leaving the arena, and she couldn't get her horse to halt opposite the correct markers. Two big faults.

"Okay. We're going to the dressage arena now to practice the steps needed for a square halt." Katherine started out of the ring, followed by the riders, one behind the other.

The dressage arena was set up on a flat area down the hill. Lauren waved to Andie, who was leading Mr. Magic around a pasture. When the riders passed by, Magic jigged sideways. His mahogany coat glistened as his muscles rippled.

"Boy, that Magic is gorgeous, isn't he?" Nicole said beside Lauren. She was a senior and had only been riding for two years. "But I sure wouldn't want to be Andie. She's going to have her hands full with him."

"Well, if anyone can handle him, it's Andie," Lauren said. "She's pretty feisty herself."

Lauren could hear Andie scolding Magic in a calm voice. Because he'd just had an operation on his eye, Andie had to hand walk him until next week. Then she could begin working him on the longe line.

When they reached the arena, Katherine had them line up by the *A* marker at the entrance.

"You'll trot into the ring, rising," she said. "About two strides before *X*—the center of the ring—sit and quietly bring your horse down to a halt. It's okay if you walk the last step or two before *X*."

Lauren listened intently to Katherine's instructions until someone schooling a horse over a fence in the outdoor ring caught her attention. She could tell by the glossy chestnut coat, white stripe, and four white feet that the horse was April Fool. Mrs. Caufield stood in the middle of the ring, calling instructions. Ashley was getting ready for tomorrow's show.

They look great, Lauren thought as Ashley steered April down a row of three practice jumps. Even though Lauren hadn't done much jumping, she could tell Ashley's position was perfect—head up, back flat and relaxed, hands resting lightly alongside April's neck. She had a confident, determined expression on her face. She was in total control.

Nothing's wrong with Ashley, Lauren told herself, feeling relieved. She'd just been imagining things. Ashley would win lots of blue ribbons at the show.

"Deepen your seat as you hold steady with your hands," Katherine was saying when Lauren tuned back in. "*Don't* lean back and *don't* pull on the reins. Lauren, you and Whisper go first."

Lauren's heart jumped. She always hated to go first. And even worse, she hadn't been listening.

"Get it together, stupid," she muttered under her breath. She had to concentrate better. She had to be motivated and in control.

If I'm going to win a ribbon at the next dressage competition, Lauren thought, *I have to be more like Ashley!*

"Admit it, Jina," Lauren said as she rode Whisper up a dirt road that wound through the woods behind the stables. "You're having a good time on the trail ride."

Jina grinned. She was riding Three Bars Jake, a chunky quarter horse. "You're right. It *is* fun. And Jake's a good guy." Reaching down, she slapped his neck fondly. "The only problem is keeping him from eating every leaf in the woods."

Lauren took a deep breath of the crisp fall air. She couldn't think of anything else she'd rather be doing.

Even Whisper was enjoying herself. She flicked her ears at fluttering leaves and shied at a flock of quail as if she were a filly again.

"Are you going to ride Applejacks next

week?" Lauren asked Jina.

"I think so. Todd's picking me up Tuesday afternoon and taking me to Middlefield Stables. It'll be weird going without Superstar, though."

When they came to a bend in the road, Lauren glanced over her shoulder. Andie, Dorothy, and Mary Beth were bringing up the rear. Andie rode Ranger, one of the school horses, and Mary Beth was riding Dan.

Next to Ranger, Dorothy was mounted on Windsor, an aged Dutch warm blood gelding. The stable manager held a lead line in her hand. The end of the lead was snapped to Dan's halter, which he wore under his bridle—just in case Mary Beth ran into trouble.

"Ready for a trot?" Andie called.

"Is it okay, Dorothy?" Lauren called back.

The stable manager nodded. "No cantering, though. I'll stay with Mary Beth."

Lauren gathered her rein as Ranger clip-clopped briskly toward them. Lauren squeezed her left leg into Whisper's side, moving her out of his path.

Neck arched, Ranger charged past, snorting loudly.

"There's no way Jake's going to keep up

with Ranger," Jina said to Lauren as the quarter horse broke into a quiet trot.

"Fine with me." Sitting deep, Lauren closed both calves around Whisper's sides. The mare moved into a smooth trot, her stride long and flowing.

As she posted, Lauren kept light contact on the reins. She could feel Whisper's mouth soften as the mare flexed her neck and her hind legs stepped briskly.

The wind blew against Lauren's cheeks as they trotted after Ranger. Whisper was so smooth, it felt as though they were flying.

Wow, Lauren thought. *If only Whisper would trot like this at the dressage competition!*

All too soon, the stables came in sight. Ranger was way ahead, walking on a loose rein. Jina and Lauren slowed their horses to a walk, too. Whisper's neck was slightly damp, but she still strode forward eagerly. When Jake caught sight of home, he pricked his ears and nickered loudly.

Lauren turned in her saddle. Behind them, the dirt road was empty. "Dorothy and Mary Beth must be pretty far back."

"Hey, look." Jina nodded toward the stable. "One of the horse vans is back from the show."

"I wonder how the Foxhall riders did," Lauren said. *I wonder how Ashley did*, she added to herself.

Jina sighed. "I wish I could have been there."

"Superstar will be better soon," Lauren said sympathetically. "Didn't Dr. Holden say you could start showing in the spring?"

"Yeah. He's going to do an ultrasound every three weeks. That way we'll know for sure how well Superstar's leg is healing."

Lauren nodded, squinting at the van parked in front of the main stable. Someone was unloading a horse wearing a hunter-green sheet and matching shipping boots.

"That looks like April Fool," Lauren said excitedly. "Ashley must be back."

Jina shrugged. "I don't care about her anymore. Now that I'm not showing Junior Hunter I guess it would be neat if Ashley won. She *is* from Foxhall, so..."

Lauren flashed her roommate a smile. "That's the spirit! Let's go see how she did."

Lauren slid off Whisper as soon as they reached the van. Missy, Ashley's friend who groomed for her at the shows, was walking April Fool around the grassy courtyard.

"How'd Ashley do?" Lauren called.

Missy gave her the thumbs-up sign. "She won the Junior Hunter Championship!"

"That's great!" Lauren squealed excitedly. "Where is she?"

Missy glanced around. "I'm not sure. Check the tack room."

Lauren looped the reins over Whisper's neck, then led her across the courtyard to the tack room. She peered inside. It was dark, and Lauren didn't see anyone. Then she heard a low moan. Cautiously, she stepped into the room. Someone was slumped on the floor. Lauren's heart pounded as she recognized Ashley's blond hair.

"Ashley! Are you all right?" she called urgently. There was no answer. Quickly, Lauren turned and looked across the courtyard. Jina was leading Jake to his stall.

"Jina!" Whipping around, Lauren clucked to Whisper, trying to get her to move. Jina glanced over her shoulder. When Jina saw Lauren jogging across the courtyard, the reins jerking on Whisper's bit, she frowned.

"What's going on?" Jina asked.

"It's Ashley," Lauren said. "Something's wrong. Hold Whisper." Thrusting the reins into

Jina's free hand, Lauren raced back to the tack room.

She hurried over to Ashley, who was lying on her side. Her friend was very pale, and her eyes were shut. Her head was propped against a tack trunk.

Lauren crouched next to her. "Ashley?" she whispered, pulse racing. Something *was* wrong. She needed to get help!

Just as Lauren turned to go for help, Ashley groaned and her eyelids fluttered open.

"Thank goodness!" Lauren gasped. "Are you all right? What happened?"

"I'm not sure." Ashley tried to struggle upright. Grasping her elbow, Lauren helped her sit up. With a weary expression, Ashley leaned back against the tack trunk.

"When I got out of the van, I felt real light-headed," she explained. "I made it into the tack room, but when I raised my arm to hang up the bridle, my legs buckled. I think I blacked out." For a moment, fear flickered in Ashley's eyes.

"Did you hit your head?" Lauren leaned sideways, trying to see.

Ashley shook her head slowly, then shut her eyes tightly as if she were in pain.

"I've got to get help," Lauren whispered, starting to rise.

"No!" Ashley said forcefully. Her fingers closed around Lauren's wrist with surprising strength. "I'm fine. Just worn out. The show was a killer."

Lauren froze, not sure what to do. Ashley didn't look fine to her. "Ashley," she pleaded, "you need help."

"No!" Ashley repeated, her gaze fierce. "Don't you tell anyone. Or I'll never forgive you."

Lauren inhaled sharply. She still thought she should go for help.

"Promise?" Ashley's fingernails dug into Lauren's wrist so hard she winced.

Anxiously, Lauren glanced at the open tack room door. She could hear Jina calling her name, asking if everything was all right.

Then she looked back at Ashley. The older girl's eyes glittered like ice. Her mouth was set in a firm line.

Lauren swallowed hard. If she told on Ashley, her new friend would hate her forever.

Slowly, Lauren nodded. "All right, Ashley. I won't tell. I promise."

"Lauren? Ashley? Are you all right in there?" Lauren heard Dorothy's calm but authoritative voice outside the tack room door.

"Help me up," Ashley hissed. "Tell them I tripped and fell."

Lauren slipped her arm around Ashley's shoulder. "We're fine," she called as Ashley staggered to her feet.

When Ashley was safely seated on top of the tack trunk, she waved Lauren over to the door. "Remember—I *tripped*," she repeated, her gaze locked on Lauren's.

Lauren nodded and hurried to the door. When she stepped outside, Dorothy was handing Windsor's reins to Andie. Jina stood beside them, holding Jake and Whisper. Behind them,

Mary Beth chewed worriedly on her lip. She was still mounted on Dan.

"What's going on?" the stable manager demanded.

Lauren opened and shut her mouth like a fish. "Um," she stammered finally, "Ashley's fine. She was just tired from the show and tripped over—um—the bridle reins."

The stable manager frowned and pulled off her helmet. Then she pushed past Lauren and strode into the tack room. Lauren could hear Ashley's shrill voice protesting that everything was all right.

Half in a daze, Lauren went over to Whisper. Jina handed her the reins.

"Are *you* okay?" Jina asked.

"Really, Lauren. You look white as a ghost," Andie said.

Lauren shook her head. "I'm okay." But she wasn't. The doubts about Ashley were flooding back. Lauren wanted to tell her roommates what had really happened. But she couldn't. She'd *promised.*

"Is this movie any good?" Mary Beth whispered to Lauren. It was Saturday night, and the four roommates were seated in the Foxhall auditorium. The large room was packed with girls eating snacks and talking. Andie sat at the end of the row, next to Jina. Mary Beth sat between Jina and Lauren.

"Are you kidding, Mary Beth?" Andie snorted. "It's a classic. There isn't any kissing or anything."

"Talk about *kissing*! Guess what?" Lauren scooted to the front of her seat so she could see Andie. "Mary Beth got a letter from a guy."

Andie's mouth fell open, and Jina stopped eating popcorn.

"Who?" Jina asked.

"A friend of mine named Brad," Mary Beth replied. "He lives near me in Cedarville."

"Oh, that hick place." Andie started to unwrap a candy bar. "Does he smell like cow manure?"

"No!" Mary Beth retorted, throwing popcorn at Andie. Scowling, she slumped down in her seat.

"Don't listen to Andie. She's just jealous," Jina told her.

Just then, the lights in the auditorium began to dim. Lauren settled in to watch the movie. But she couldn't stop thinking about

Ashley. After dinner, she had called Mill Hall to see if her friend was okay. The girl who answered the phone said there was a do-not-disturb sign hanging on Ashley's doorknob.

Suddenly, a spotlight lit up the stage, and Mr. Frawley, the headmaster of Foxhall Academy, stepped in front of a microphone.

"Good evening, ladies," he said, his voice ringing out over the room. "I have an announcement."

Lauren sat up in alarm. Was it something about Ashley?

"We hope you enjoy tonight's program," Mr. Frawley went on. "But before we go to our feature movie, we'll be showing a short film called *Growing Up*."

Lauren heard Andie groan loudly.

"After the movie, Dr. Stein will be available to answer questions," the headmaster continued. "Dr. Stein is a well-known psychologist who deals daily with teenagers and their problems. Dr. Stein, will you stand up, please?"

A small, gray-haired woman in the front row stood up. She smiled and bobbed her head at the audience. Seconds later, the spotlight faded.

The movie wasn't too bad, but Lauren had

seen one just like it last year at her old school. A few girls giggled in parts, but most of them just looked bored. Lauren couldn't really concentrate, either.

She kept thinking about Ashley.

Ten minutes later, the screen went black and the lights brightened.

"That was a waste of time," Jina said as she crumpled up her popcorn bag. "I hate all that you're-growing-up-now stuff."

Mary Beth stood up and stretched. "All I wanted to find out about was kissing."

"Why don't you practice with your horse, Dan," Andie joked. "I bet he's better looking than Brad."

"He is not!" Mary Beth exclaimed. This time, she threw her entire popcorn bag at her. Andie caught it and tossed it right back. Laughing, Mary Beth and Jina both dodged the flying bag. It hit Lauren's leg.

"Hey," Lauren protested. The bag plopped on the floor. Kernels spilled everywhere.

"Now look what you did, Andie," Mary Beth said.

"You started it!" Andie shot back.

Abruptly, Lauren stood up. She'd suddenly had a great idea. "I'll see you guys later," she said as she made her way down the row of seats.

"You can't just leave," Mary Beth said. "Don't you want to see *International Velvet*? Where are you going?"

"None of your business," Lauren said.

"Can't we come with you?" Mary Beth persisted.

"No!" Lauren whirled to face her roommates. Mary Beth looked startled. Andie and Jina were staring at Lauren, too.

"It's personal," Lauren explained. "Okay?"

Mary Beth nodded hesitantly. "Okay."

When Lauren reached the aisle, she pushed through the crowd of girls milling around the auditorium. Dr. Stein, the psychologist, was answering questions on the stage. *It's not the most private way to do this,* Lauren thought. But she had to ask her about Ashley. Dr. Stein wasn't a faculty member. She'd be the perfect person to talk to.

Slowly, Lauren approached the stage. When most of the girls had started back to their seats, she went up to Dr. Stein.

"Uh, I have a question to ask you, Dr. Stein," Lauren stammered. "But, um..." She glanced back at the row where her roommates had been sitting, but her view was blocked by the other students moving around the auditorium.

Dr. Stein smiled warmly and checked her watch. "The main movie is about to start. Mr. Frawley told me eight-thirty. Would you like to go somewhere private to talk?"

"Oh yes," Lauren said gratefully.

"Why don't we walk out to the lovely garden Mr. Frawley showed me on my tour," Dr. Stein said.

Lauren nodded. She followed Dr. Stein off the stage and out into the hall that led to Old House. She still hadn't seen her roommates.

They're probably mad at me now, Lauren thought. Not that she blamed them. She'd been pretty snotty to them.

The garden was chilly, but gold and purple chrysanthemums still bloomed under a dogwood tree. Dr. Stein sat down on a bench. Feeling awkward and shy, Lauren sat on the end farthest from her.

"What can I help you with?" the doctor asked, her smile kind. "Don't worry—I've heard every question there is."

"Well, um." Lauren stared down at her hands clutched in her lap. "I don't have a question. But I do have a friend who's acting really strange. I think something's wrong, but I'm not sure what."

"What is she doing that seems strange?"

Lauren frowned. Now that she thought about it, Ashley's exercising and worrying about her weight weren't all that strange. Would Dr. Stein laugh at her?

Lauren bit her lip. "The other day, after a horse show, this friend of mine passed out. When I went to get help, she made me promise just to tell people she tripped."

Dr. Stein nodded solemnly. "Why do you think she passed out?"

"Well." Lauren took a deep breath. Tears pricked her eyes. Then in one long sentence, she told Dr. Stein everything. It felt so good to let it all out that she couldn't stop.

When Lauren was done, Dr. Stein patted her hand. "Good job. It sounds as though you've noticed something that your friend has been hiding."

"I have?"

"Yes. It's possible that your friend has an eating disorder."

"Eating disorder?" Lauren repeated, feeling relieved. "That doesn't sound so terrible."

Dr. Stein frowned. "That's not true. Your friend may be suffering from anorexia. It's a disease in which the person slowly starves himself or herself. It can be very serious. Fifteen percent of anorexics die of complications of the disease."

Die! Lauren leaped up. Dr. Stein was crazy. Ashley wasn't sick enough to die.

"You're wrong," Lauren blurted out. "My friend doesn't have an eating disorder. Just forget everything I said!"

Lauren whirled around and raced for the door.

"Wait!" Dr. Stein called. "I didn't mean to scare you! I—"

But Lauren was already in the door. She ran so fast, she collided with several girls coming down the hall. One of them grabbed her arm.

"Whoa, little sis."

Lauren looked up. It was Stephanie. She was surrounded by a group of older girls. Some of them were Ashley's friends, too.

"What's wrong?" Stephanie asked.

Lauren glanced over her shoulder. Any second Dr. Stein would rush through the doorway into the hall, babbling about eating disorders. Then everyone would find out what she'd told her.

"Nothing! I've got to find my roommates."

Yanking her arm from her sister's grasp, Lauren ran down the long hall. She had to get back to the suite. She had to be alone.

Pushing through the double doors at the end of the hall, she tore down the steps of Old House and across the drive. She didn't slow down until she was halfway across the courtyard.

"Stupid, stupid," Lauren muttered angrily as she gasped for breath. Not only had she broken her promise to Ashley, but she'd blabbed everything to Dr. Stein. At least she hadn't mentioned Ashley's name. Or her own.

Lauren began to relax a bit as she trudged slowly toward Bracken Hall. Maybe Dr. Stein wouldn't tell anyone else. Maybe she'd forget the whole thing.

Maybe.

Lauren stared at the sheet of paper. *Training Level, Test 2* was written at the top. It was Monday afternoon, and all the Foxhall riders going to the dressage competition at Hunting Horn Farms had met in the stable office. After a short lecture on competition rules, Katherine had passed out the different tests they'd each perform on Saturday.

As Lauren read through the beginning movements of her test, her brain began to grow numb.

1. *A* Enter working trot sitting
   X Halt, salute, proceed working trot sitting
2. C Track right
   M Working trot rising
   B Circle left 20 m
   F Working trot sitting

Lauren skimmed through the rest of the test. There were eighteen movements in all! She groaned. It was worse than math. She'd never remember them.

Last summer at the clinic, someone had stood by the side of the arena and called out the movements. But early on, Katherine had told all of them that no readers would be allowed. Part of competing would be learning the tests.

Tears of frustration welled in Lauren's eyes. No matter how hard she practiced, she'd be so nervous she'd forget everything when she rode into the arena.

Unless—

Lauren gripped the paper so tightly that it

crumpled. Maybe Ashley could help her. She could help her memorize the movements! Then Lauren's heart sank. Her math midterm was Friday. That was important, too. Could she do both?

"Is everything all right, Lauren?" someone asked.

Startled, Lauren jerked up her head. Katherine was staring down at her. The rest of the girls had already left the office.

"Uh, yeah," Lauren stammered as she folded up the test.

Katherine nodded. "Good. I thought maybe you had a question. Everyone else has gone to get their horses tacked up. We're practicing circles this afternoon."

Now Lauren felt stupid. She was probably the only one who was worried about the test. "Um, I do have one question. What happens if you forget part of the test?"

"If you go off course, the judge will give you two penalty points," Katherine explained. "Then he'll blow a whistle, stop you, and get you back on track. If you make another kind of error—like rise at the trot instead of sit—the judge will also deduct two points."

Lauren grimaced. "Great. By the end of my

test, I'll have a million penalty points."

Katherine laughed. "Maybe this time. But if you continue to rely on a reader, you'll never learn the tests. Right?"

"Right," Lauren agreed reluctantly.

"Now go get Whisper," Katherine said. "We have lots to do this week."

When Lauren left the office, the bright October sun made her feel better. She grabbed Whisper's halter, lead line, and grooming kit from the tack room, then headed for April Fool's stall. She'd ask Ashley right now about helping her tonight.

When she reached the stall, April stuck her nose over the bottom of the Dutch door.

"Hey, girl." Lauren slid her fingers down the horse's velvety nose, then poked her own head into the stall. Ashley was on the mare's left side, brushing her. April's chestnut coat gleamed.

"She's looking good," Lauren said. "How come you're not riding today?"

Ashley backed April up, then walked around the mare's head to the right side. "April's on vacation. She's pooped after the show."

Just then Ashley turned to face Lauren.

Lauren couldn't believe how awful she looked.

The older girl had huge circles under her eyes. Her blond hair was pulled into a tight ponytail, emphasizing her sharp cheekbones, and her petite body looked lost in an extra-large sweatshirt.

"Maybe you need a vacation, too," Lauren said without thinking.

"What do you mean?" Ashley snapped, her blue eyes narrowing.

Lauren didn't know what to say. How did you tell someone she looked terrible?

"I mean, you seemed kind of tired on Saturday when you passed out—"

"Hey!" Ashley cut in. "I didn't pass out. I tripped." Stepping up to the door, she stuck her pale face close to Lauren's. "Remember?"

Lauren drew back. "I remember," she whispered. It was a good thing she hadn't given Dr. Stein any names. Ashley would have definitely been furious.

Bending down, Ashley picked a mane comb from her grooming box. "Did you want something?" she asked, her tone suddenly pleasant.

"Well, yes." Lauren told Ashley about the dressage test.

"Sure, I'd love to help you," Ashley said

brightly. "So quit worrying. Learning those movements will be a piece of cake. Just like decimals."

Lauren breathed a sigh of relief. "Thanks, Ash. You're the greatest. I'll see you tonight."

Lauren waved, then went to Whisper's stall. The mare was snoozing in the back corner. When Lauren unlatched the door, the mare's head popped around, and she nickered softly.

"Hey, my pretty." Lauren stuck her hand in her jean's pocket and pulled out a few carrot sticks. Holding them on her palm, she fed them to Whisper. The mare picked them up with her soft lips and crunched them noisily.

"Now don't tell anyone," Lauren murmured into Whisper's ear. "You know what an old poop Mrs. Caufield is about feeding you treats."

"Hey, Lauren," a voice called from outside the stall.

"I won't do it again!" Lauren croaked as she spun around, expecting to see an angry Mrs. Caufield.

But it was only Mary Beth.

Lauren clutched her chest. "You scared me!" she breathed.

Her roommate laughed. "Sneaking Whisper carrots again?"

Lauren nodded. "Did you just get to the stables?"

"Yeah. I wanted to tell you there was a message for you on our door."

"Who was it from?"

"Mr. Lyons. He's your counselor, right? He wants to see you before dinner."

"He does?" Lauren squeaked, her heart plunging to her toes.

Oh no. Dr. Stein must have figured out who she was. Now Lyons probably wanted to find out who her mysterious friend was that had the mysterious illness.

"Lauren? Are you all right?" Mary Beth asked, leaning over the Dutch door.

Slowly, Lauren shook her head. "No. I'm not all right. I'm in *big* trouble."

"What are you talking about?" Mary Beth asked, frowning at Lauren. "Why are you in big trouble?"

"I can't tell you." Lauren hooked the lead line onto Whisper's halter, afraid to look at her roommate.

"Why are you being so secretive?" Mary Beth asked. "Are you flunking math again? Is that why Mr. Lyons wants to see you?"

"No," Lauren said forcefully. "And I mean it when I say I don't want to talk about it."

Mary Beth looked hurt. "You don't have to be so snotty. You know, ever since you started hanging around with Ashley, you've been acting just like her."

Lauren turned away. She couldn't tell anyone else about Ashley. It was too risky, and she'd already broken her promise once. Picking up the dandy brush, she started whisking caked manure from Whisper's side.

"Okay. Don't explain," Mary Beth said, stomping off. "See if I care," she threw over her shoulder.

Tears pricked Lauren's eyes. *I'm sorry, Mary Beth,* she wanted to call after her friend. But she only brushed harder. If she didn't hurry she'd be late for her lesson.

"These cones mark out a twenty-meter circle," Katherine explained a few minutes later to the four mounted riders walking their horses in the ring. "I want you to memorize its size. You must be able to see and feel that circle. Your horse's body must bend to the inside, conforming to the shape. That means if you're tracking left, your left leg is on the girth, your right leg slightly behind the girth."

"Track left, bend slightly," Lauren repeated as Whisper strode counterclockwise around the outside of the cones. "Left leg behind the girth—no, right leg," she corrected herself. Hastily, she shifted her right leg back where it belonged, nudging Whisper's side by accident.

Immediately, the mare broke into a trot.

"We're walking, Lauren," Katherine called.

"I know, I know," Lauren muttered, pulling back on the reins. Raising her nose in the air, Whisper quickened her pace, trying to get away from the harsh feel of the bit.

Frustrated, Lauren tugged harder. Whisper tossed her head before slowing to a stiff-legged walk.

"Lauren!" Katherine scolded. "No jerking on that horse's mouth!"

"Sorry," Lauren said. Bending over Whisper's mane, she stroked the mare's neck. "I'm sorry, Whisper," she told her. "I owe you an apple."

"Now, let's get back to circles," Katherine continued.

Circles. Think about circles, Lauren told herself as she straightened in the saddle.

In Saturday's dressage test, she would have to ride four twenty-meter circles. Lauren knew how important it was to make them the right size.

She had to relax and concentrate.

She had to forget about her meeting with Mr. Lyons.

She had to forget about Ashley.

"You wanted to see me, Mr. Lyons?" Lauren asked, her voice a whisper. She stood in the office doorway, clutching her riding helmet. Mr. Lyons, one of Foxhall's gym teachers and soccer coaches, sat behind his desk, talking to Mrs. Zelinski, the school nurse.

"Come on in, Lauren," he said. Mr. Lyons stood up and gestured for her to enter. The nurse gave Lauren a wave, then disappeared into another office.

As Lauren walked in, she couldn't help but notice how handsome Mr. Lyons was with his wavy blond hair, long lashes, and baby blue eyes. He looked like a movie star.

No wonder Ashley had a crush on him.

"Have a seat." Mr. Lyons pulled a chair up for her, then sat down behind his desk again.

Lauren slid into the chair. Immediately, she noticed the manure on the soles of her boots.

"I came straight from riding," she apologized, tucking her feet under the rungs of the chair.

"That's all right. You're not the first." Mr. Lyons picked up a pen and started to fiddle with it. "I wanted to talk to you today about several things, Lauren." He paused and cleared his throat.

"First, I want to congratulate you," he began. "Mrs. Jacquin says you've pulled your math grade up to a C. I guess you and Ashley make a great team."

Ashley. Lauren fidgeted anxiously in her seat. Did he know about her conversation with Dr. Stein?

"Now we just have to get you through the midterm."

Lauren bobbed her head nervously. "I think I'll pass it."

"Good. Now, there's another matter I need to discuss with you." He cleared his throat again, and Lauren's stomach churned.

Saliva rose in her throat, and her eyes watered. Holding her helmet tightly against her stomach, she hunched over in the chair.

"Are you okay?" Mr. Lyons asked.

"Yes," Lauren lied. She tried to stop the tears welling in her eyes from spilling down her cheeks, but it was no use. "No. I'm not okay," she whispered hoarsely. "I told Dr. Stein something I shouldn't have! I broke my promise to Ashley!"

Dropping his pen, Mr. Lyons quickly pulled

a tissue from a box and handed it to her.

Lauren blew her nose. "Oh no, I can't believe I told you her name. I'm such a dope."

"I already know about Ashley, Lauren," he said gently.

"You do?" Lauren sniffed, raising her head.

He nodded. "I saw Ashley this morning to touch base with her about her junior service project. I hadn't seen her in a week. She didn't look well at all. Right away I guessed that Ashley was the friend whom you discussed with Dr. Stein."

Slowly, Lauren sat up straight. "But I never told Dr. Stein my name. And she said it was a private conversation," she added angrily.

"It wasn't easy for Dr. Stein to betray your confidence," Mr. Lyons explained. "But she was very concerned. As she told you, an eating disorder is very serious. From what you were saying about your friend, she felt that one of our students might be in danger. She went to Mr. Frawley, and they looked through all the student files." Mr. Lyons smiled. "Dr. Stein picked you out right away."

Reaching across the desk, Lauren plucked another tissue from the box. "Then Mr. Frawley came to you because he knows you are my counselor?"

Mr. Lyons nodded. "Right. He was hoping you'd confide in me. Lauren, believe me, you've done the right thing. Now Ashley can get help."

Lauren sighed in relief. Her stomach had stopped churning. "What happens now?"

"Mrs. Zelinski is waiting to talk with both of us. Is that okay?"

"I guess so."

Before Mr. Lyons even stood up, the nurse bustled in.

"Dear, you did the right thing," Mrs. Zelinski told Lauren, patting her on the shoulder. "People with eating disorders are very good at hiding their problems. Sometimes they don't even realize they're ill. You were smart to notice something was wrong and very brave to talk to Dr. Stein."

Lauren glanced from the nurse to Mr. Lyons. "But how do you know for sure it's an eating disorder? I mean, Dr. Stein said people with anorexia could die. Ashley's not that sick. I know she isn't!"

Mrs. Zelinski patted Lauren's hand. "There,

there. She may not have an eating disorder. It's our job to find out. Tomorrow morning, I've scheduled Ashley for a routine exam with Dr. Helmut. He's our visiting physician. If there's a problem, we'll call her parents right away."

"The important thing is, you can stop worrying about Ashley, Lauren," Mr. Lyons assured her. "The school will handle everything now."

"And you won't tell her I was the one who told her secret?" Lauren asked anxiously.

"Absolutely not. I'll take the blame for noticing. It'll be my problem from now on." Mr. Lyons smiled warmly, his blue eyes crinkling at the corners. Lauren almost melted.

"Thanks," she said, swallowing hard. Things had worked out better than she hoped.

Ashley would be okay now, Lauren told herself.

Everything would be okay.

"See? I told you it'd be easy," Ashley said to Lauren that night.

They'd finished Lauren's math homework and studied for Friday's midterm. Then, using the Common Room chairs, the two of them had marked out a pretend dressage arena.

"Here's *A*, the entrance to the arena," Ashley continued, pointing to the space between two folding chairs which they'd placed about a foot apart.

"According to the test, you enter at a 'working trot sitting.'" Ashley looked up and shook her head. "Whatever that is. *Achoo!*"

The sneeze was so loud, Lauren jumped. Ashley's nose was bright red from blowing.

Lauren was relieved that Ashley was seeing the doctor tomorrow. She didn't dare say that to Ashley, though. Her friend might suspect something.

"Are you sure you don't want to do this tomorrow?" Lauren asked for the tenth time. "You should be in bed."

Ashley waved a tissue in the air. "No way. I feel fine. Penny and I still have to lift weights tonight. I have two weeks left to strengthen my arms before the next show." She slapped her thighs under her sweatpants. "And lose those five pounds I probably gained Sunday from lying around all day. *Achoo!*"

She blew her nose, then flapped the test paper at Lauren. "Okay, now I'll read the test while you go through it movement by movement."

Lauren couldn't help but grin. Ashley had thought up a great plan to teach her the test. Now she could practice for the dressage competition every night—without a horse.

She just hoped no one came into Mill Hall's Common Room. They'd think she was crazy trotting from chair *H* to chair *F*.

When study hour was over, the girls called it quits. Lauren rearranged the furniture, putting the last chair back just as another girl came into the room. It was Penny, Ashley's roommate.

"Hey, Ash!" Penny greeted her friend as she headed toward the snack machine. Penny had broad shoulders and a chunky build, exactly the opposite of Ashley. "Ready to work out?"

"Sure." Ashley grimaced when Penny pulled a bag of potato chips from the snack machine. "Those are pure grease and salt."

Penny grinned and waved the bag in the air. "I need them for energy if we're lifting weights." She flexed her arm, bulging out a muscle. "Nice, huh?"

Lauren gathered up her books from the sofa.

"If I don't see you tomorrow, maybe we can practice Wednesday," she said to Ashley.

"Why wouldn't I see you tomorrow?" Ashley asked, frowning.

Lauren wanted to smack herself. Why had she said a dumb thing like that? "Your cold might be worse," she fibbed.

"Nah," Ashley said with a wave. "It'll be gone by then, you'll see."

"Okay. 'Bye." Grabbing her jacket, Lauren hurried out of the Common Room.

That was close. Lauren left Mill Hall and jogged down the sidewalk. The night was chilly, and she was eager to get back to the suite. It seemed like ages since she'd just hung out with her roommates.

When she walked into the suite, Mary Beth was sitting at her desk, busily writing. Jina and Andie were out.

"Doing homework?" Lauren asked Mary Beth as she dropped her books on her bed.

"No," Mary Beth said sharply, hiding the paper with her arms.

Uh-oh. She's still mad at me, Lauren thought.

"Look, I'm sorry about this afternoon," she said. "Maybe by tomorrow I'll be able to tell you what's going on."

"Oh?" Mary Beth raised one brow. "Is Ashley giving you permission to talk to us again?"

Lauren flushed. "That's not fair, Mary Beth."

Mary Beth shrugged. "Well, I hate secrets, and you've been keeping lots of them."

"From *everybody,*" Lauren said. Turning, she threw herself facedown on the bed. "Not just you," she muttered into her bedspread.

"What do you mean?" Mary Beth asked. Lauren heard the scrape of her desk chair.

Then the mattress sagged as Mary Beth sat next to her. "You said you were in big trouble. Is it because of something Ashley did?"

"Sort of," Lauren mumbled. She flipped onto her back. "I can't say anything more. But it's not about you or Jina or Andie. Honest."

Mary Beth studied her for a moment. "Okay. I believe you. But I *can* keep a secret, Lauren."

"I know." Lauren sighed.

Mary Beth grinned. "Can *you* keep a secret?"

Lauren nodded.

Mary Beth jumped off the bed and rushed over to her desk. "Guess who I'm writing to," she said, grabbing the piece of paper.

"Brad!" Lauren cried gleefully.

"Yup." Mary Beth clutched the sheet to her chest. "I'm inviting him to come to Foxhall with my parents for Parents' Weekend next month."

"Cool!" Lauren sat up, excitedly. She was so happy she and Mary Beth were friends again. "Do you think he'll come?"

"I hope so."

Lauren stood up and took her bathroom bucket from the top of her dresser. "I know something that might convince him."

"What?" Mary Beth peered eagerly over her shoulder.

"This!" Lauren held up a small bottle. "Bath scent. We'll sprinkle a little on the letter. Brad won't be able to stay away!"

On Tuesday, Lauren stood in the hall after her last class, waiting for Ashley to come out of English. She was going to tell Ashley she had a question about a math problem. But really she just wanted to see if Ashley would say anything about her doctor's appointment that morning.

Mr. Vassaloti, Ashley's advanced math teacher, was keeping the girls past the bell. Lauren peered around the doorway. She could see Penny and a few other juniors and seniors whom she didn't know. Ashley wasn't in the room.

A tiny blade of fear stabbed Lauren's heart. *Where was she?*

Finally, Mr. Vassaloti dismissed the small class. Lauren tapped Penny's arm as the older girl stepped into the hall.

"Where's Ashley?" she asked anxiously.

"In the infirmary," Penny told her.

“Is she all right?”

“Yeah. It’s just the flu. But you know old Zelinski. She thinks every sneeze is a major health crisis.” Penny waved to a friend. “Why don’t you go visit her? Tell her I said hi,” she added as she took off down the hall.

Lauren checked the clock over the door. If she hurried, she could visit Ashley and still make her riding lesson.

Lauren jogged down the hall and out the door of the math and science building. The infirmary was upstairs in Old House.

But when she reached the second floor, Lauren paused. Her heart was pounding, and it wasn’t just from running up the stairs. What if the doctor had told Ashley she did have an eating disorder? How would she take it?

Lauren took a deep breath, then pushed open the door. Mrs. Zelinski sat at her desk. A telephone receiver was stuck between her ear and shoulder, leaving her hands free to fold linens. “Unh-huh, unh-huh,” she was saying into the phone.

Lauren waved. “I’m here to see Ashley,” she whispered.

The nurse nodded toward a curtain partition.

Lauren approached the bed on tiptoes. When she peeked around the partition, she caught her breath. Ashley was so tiny, she hardly made a bulge in the blanket.

Her eyes were closed, her breathing labored. Lauren was about to turn away, when Ashley coughed harshly. Opening her eyes, the older girl pulled one arm from under the blanket and reached for a glass of chipped ice. Lauren rushed over to get it for her.

"Hi," she said, holding out the glass.

Ashley's hand froze in the air. Then, her eyes widened with fury. "What are *you* doing here?"

Startled, Lauren almost dropped the glass. "I came to visit you."

"Why?" Ashley demanded, struggling to sit up. "So you could tell more lies about me?"

Lauren backed away. "What do you mean?"

"You're the only one who knew I blacked out after the show." Pushing herself up on one elbow, Ashley pointed a skinny finger at Lauren. "You broke your promise!"

Lauren set the glass back on the bedside table, her hand shaking. Tears stung her eyes. "I'm sorry, Ashley. I was just so worried about you."

"There's nothing to worry about. You stuck your nose into my business for no reason. I'm *not* sick. I'm *not* too thin." Sweat dotted Ashley's brow, and her blond hair stuck out like dry straw. "But, because of you, the school's telling my parents all your crazy lies."

"But, Ashley," Lauren pleaded, "can't you see? You *are* sick!"

Ashley's eyes narrowed. "*You're* the one who's sick, poking your nose where it didn't belong. Get out, Lauren. Out!" she screamed in a croak.

"O-okay," Lauren stammered, nodding as she backed away again. Blinking back tears, she spun around and ran past a worried-looking Mrs. Zelinski.

"You've ruined my life!" Lauren heard Ashley yell as she raced out the door. "I'll never forgive you, Lauren Remick. *Never!*"

Lauren ran across the courtyard, her chest heaving with choked-down sobs.

"Lauren!" someone shouted. "Aren't you going to your riding lesson?"

Glancing up, Lauren saw Andie, Jina, and Mary Beth heading toward the stables. Her roommates wore their riding boots and carried helmets.

Lauren slowed long enough to blurt, "I can't. Tell Katherine I'm sick."

"Sick?" Lauren heard Mary Beth repeat. But she didn't stop to explain. She didn't want to talk to anyone, not even her friends.

When she reached Bracken Hall, Lauren tore up to the fourth floor, slamming the door behind her. She threw herself on her bed and buried her nose in her pillow.

If only Mom were here, Lauren thought miserably. She'd made that same wish several times since she'd arrived at Foxhall. But this time she really meant it.

"Lauren?" The door opened, and Stephanie poked her head into the suite. "Hey, what's wrong?" She came over and sat on the bed. "Christina saw you charging into the dorm like a crazy person." Stephanie patted Lauren's back soothingly. "Are you all right?"

Lauren shook her head. Stephanie handed her a tissue.

"Tell me what's going on," Stephanie said. She almost sounded like their mother.

Lauren hesitated. Stephanie knew Ashley pretty well. But Lauren didn't care anymore. She needed to confide in someone.

"Oh, Steph, I really blew it." Lauren sat up and hugged her pillow to herself. Then, wiping her eyes, she told her sister everything.

For a while, Stephanie was quiet. Then she shook her head, her silky blond hair whipping back and forth against her shoulders. "You sure did mess up," she said.

Lauren's mouth fell open. "Well, thanks for all the sympathy. I'm your sister, remember?"

"Oh, come on, Lauren." Stephanie stood up

and walked over to the window. "Don't you know rule number one around here? It's called mind your own business. Ashley isn't anorexic. Lots of girls worry constantly about looking great." She brushed back the curtain and peered out into the courtyard. "Ashley just took things a little too far."

Turning, she glared down at her sister. "But *you* tattled."

Lauren shrank from Stephanie's accusing eyes.

"I've got to meet Christina. She's waiting for me outside." In two strides, Stephanie reached the door. "I just hope you never rat on *me*," she said over her shoulder. Then, yanking open the door, she left.

Lauren's brain felt numb. Her own sister had betrayed her!

Curling up on her side, she clutched the pillow tightly. No one was on her side. *No one.*

"Hey, Remick, feeling better?" Andie asked Lauren as she burst through the suite door a few hours later. Flicking on the lights, she marched across the room to her own bed.

Lauren blinked sleepily. "I must have fallen asleep," she murmured.

Andie jerked off her riding boots. They fell on the floor with a loud *clunk*. "Are you going to dinner?"

Lauren yawned. "I guess so."

Andie studied her a moment. "Then you can't be too sick."

Lauren sighed. "No. It's more like a super-bad dream."

"You mean about Ashley and all." Andie snorted. "Serves her right."

Lauren sat up. "What did you hear about Ashley?"

"The whole school knows by now that she's anorexic. I mean, like, *big surprise*. I could have told that brain surgeon Mrs. Zelinski what was wrong with Ashley. She didn't have to call in a special doctor."

"How do you know so much about anorexia?" Lauren asked.

Andie slid her T-shirt over her head and stuffed it in her laundry bag. The shirt was covered with horsehair. "Two girls had eating disorders at my old school. One was a lot like Ashley. The other was bulimic. She'd snarf down food like a pig, then throw up."

"Why didn't you tell me about Ashley?" Lauren demanded. "Then I wouldn't have had to talk to Dr. Stein about everything."

Andie shrugged. Reaching into her dresser, she pulled out a white turtleneck. "It wasn't any of my business."

"That's what Stephanie said," Lauren muttered, slumping onto her bed again. "So where are Jina and Mary Beth?"

Maybe they'll still be my friends, she told herself glumly.

"Jina went to Middlefield with Todd to ride that new pony—Rotten Apple or whatever his name is."

Lauren couldn't help giggling. "It's Applejacks."

"And Mary Beth always takes two hours to cool Dan off after her lesson."

"That's 'cause he's so big." Lauren sighed and rolled over on her stomach. "Did anyone even wonder where I was?"

"Yeah. Katherine said since you missed today's lesson, you weren't going to the dressage competition."

Lauren snapped to attention. "What?"

"Just kidding." Andie grinned.

"Jerk." Lauren made a face at her.

"You'd better get dressed for dinner," Andie said, putting on her blue Foxhall blazer.

Lauren twisted her long braid. "I'm skipping dinner."

"Why?" Andie challenged. "Are you afraid all Ashley's friends will call you a tattletale?"

"Something like that," Lauren mumbled.

"Well, forget it. Ashley doesn't have any friends."

"What do you mean?" Lauren asked.

"A real friend would have told someone about Ashley," Andie explained. "She wouldn't have let her starve to death. You are the only friend she had."

Lauren's eyes widened. "You mean that?"

Andie tossed her mane of hair behind her shoulders. "Sure. Ashley will hate you for it. But, like I said before, who cares? Don't let it get you down. Mary Beth, Jina, and I think you did okay."

Lauren grinned. "Thanks, Andie."

Andie nodded. "Right. So are you coming to dinner or what?"

"Yeah." Jumping off the bed, Lauren crossed over to the wardrobe and pulled out the white blouse she wore under her own blazer. "I'm glad you guys are on my side. That really means a lot."

"Well, don't get mushy about it," Andie

said, tying the laces of her tennis shoes. "And if the other girls start giving you grief, don't worry. I'll back you up. This dopey school needs a good food fight."

Ten minutes later, Andie, Lauren, and Mary Beth were walking across the courtyard toward the cafeteria. Dark shadows loomed across the grass.

"Jina said she'll meet us there," Mary Beth told the others. "Todd and Mrs. Caufield are talking to her about showing Applejacks this weekend."

"Then she won't be able to come to my dressage competition," Lauren said, pouting.

Andie rolled her eyes. "Oh, come on, Lauren. That dressage stuff is s-o-o-o boring. I mean, every horse does the same thing—walk to one letter, trot to another, then you salute some stupid judge."

Lauren bristled at Andie. "Well, what *you're* doing isn't exactly thrilling, either," she retorted. "Magic just goes around and around in a circle when you longe him."

"Well, we won't be doing that much longer," Andie shot back. She stopped and put her hands on her hips. "Magic's going to be a jumper. *That's* exciting."

"Hey, Remick!" a sharp voice interrupted.

Penny stood on the sidewalk, her legs planted in a fighter's stance. Her mouth was pulled down in a scowl. Two other girls Lauren had seen before at Mill Hall stood next to Penny, blocking the steps.

Lauren gulped. "What?"

"Did you hear the latest news about your good friend Ashley?" Penny asked.

Lauren shook her head.

"Her parents put her in the county hospital. They're feeding her through tubes, and some shrink wants her to tell him all her problems."

"Oh," Lauren squeaked.

Penny stepped closer, loomed over her. "She called me as soon as she got there. You're allowed one call before they lock you up."

Lauren's gaze darted to Mary Beth, then Andie. Both of her roommates were staring at Penny in shocked silence.

"So what else did Ashley say?" Lauren practically whispered.

"She said to give you a message," Penny said. She raised one arm, her fingers clenched tightly in a fist. "And *this* is it."

Lauren drew back from Penny's upraised arm. But before Penny could do anything, Andie jumped in between them.

"Pick on somebody your own size, Benny," Andie snapped. She was a foot smaller than Penny and half as wide.

"It's *Penny,*" the older girl said, her brows coming together in a V.

Andie stood on tiptoes so her nose almost touched the other girl's. Her hair seemed to bristle like the fur on a mad cat's back. "You look like a Benny to me."

"Penny!" one of her friends hissed. "A teacher's coming."

Penny quickly lowered her fist. "Good. I didn't want to smash these twerps." Her gaze went from Andie to Lauren. "You got the message, Remick, right?"

"Right," Lauren croaked.

The three older girls turned and went up the steps.

"'Bye, *Benny,*" Andie called sweetly as the doors shut behind them.

"Whew." Mary Beth let out a loud gasp. "That was close. I thought she was going to flatten you guys."

Andie snorted. "Nah. It was all a big bluff."

"Well, she had *me* scared," Lauren admitted. "Thanks for coming to my rescue, Andie."

Just then Jina jogged across the courtyard.

"Hi, guys. Thanks for waiting up," she said when she reached the steps.

Mary Beth caught her arm. "You just missed the most awesome spectacle," she said excitedly.

Jina raised her brows. "I did?"

"Yup. Andie and Lauren fought off three upper-class students the size of those statues outside the library."

"They did?" Jina said doubtfully, glancing from Andie to Lauren.

"Well, Andie did anyway." Lauren laughed

weakly. "Mary Beth will tell you all about it," she added as she headed up the steps to the cafeteria. "My stomach's still in knots!"

"Dan-divide, Mary-multiply, Superstar-subtract," Lauren murmured to herself a few days later. She was hunched over her math midterm, chewing on her pencil eraser as she recited the steps for dividing decimals.

Quickly, she jotted down the steps in the margin of her test. It was three pages long, with a hundred problems. And since Ashley hadn't helped her since Monday, Lauren knew she was going to flunk—big time.

She squeezed her eyes tightly, trying to recall the trick Ashley had taught her about comparing decimals. But all she could see was Ashley screaming that she'd never forgive her.

She hadn't heard from Ashley. None of Ashley's "friends" were talking to her, either. Even Stephanie was ignoring her. That really hurt. And Mr. Lyons and Mrs. Zelinski had said Ashley was fine, but they couldn't discuss any more because it was confidential.

Lauren chomped down on her eraser, biting it in two. *Concentrate*, she scolded herself. *Forget Ashley. Just do your best. Then it will be over and you can get ready for the dressage competition tomorrow. Unless, of course, you flunk.*

Lauren groaned. What a disaster that competition was going to be. Her roommates had drilled her every night on the sequence of movements in the dressage test. She'd walked, trotted, and cantered them twenty times in the arena they'd set up in the Common Room.

But by tomorrow, she'd probably forget them.

"Lauren," Mrs. Jacquin whispered behind her. "Remember, if you're stuck on a problem, move to the next one. Then come back."

What if you're stuck on all the problems? Lauren wanted to ask. Instead, she nodded and jotted down the first answer that popped into her head. Maybe, by some miracle, it would be right.

"This is the last braid," Lauren told Jina. It was early Saturday morning, and the two girls were finishing up Whisper's mane at Hunting Horn Farms. Standing on an overturned bucket by Whisper's withers, Lauren looped navy yarn around the end of the braid, then knotted it. "I think my fingers are numb," she added.

Jina began combing out Whisper's tail.

"What fingers?" she joked.

Using an embroidery needle, Lauren threaded a loop of yarn into the base of the braid. She yanked the yarn, doubling the braid under, then knotted it tight.

Finally, using small nail scissors, she clipped off the loose ends of yarn from all the braids, working her way up Whisper's mane to her ears. Whisper shook her head, bored and restless. She'd been standing quietly, munching hay from a net, for almost two hours.

"She looks great," Jina said.

Standing back, the girls checked out their handiwork. Whisper's copper-colored coat gleamed, her tail flowed thick and soft, and the neat braids accented her gracefully arched neck.

"Thanks for helping," Lauren said. "I can't believe she got so dirty after her bath yesterday."

"No problem."

Lauren sighed. "Now I see why you got all stressed out before your shows. I was so nervous I couldn't sleep last night."

She smiled shyly at Jina. "I'm glad you didn't end up riding Applejacks at a show today," she added.

"Me too," Jina said. "It's kind of fun watching someone else go through all this hassle. Do you have everything in Whisper's grooming kit?"

Lauren nodded.

"Gloves, riding coat—?"

"Mary Beth's bringing them."

"Extra saddle pad, towels—?"

"Already packed."

Jina gave Lauren a high-five. "Then I guess you're ready!"

"When's your ride time?" Andie asked as she saddled Whisper a few hours later. Lauren was wiping off her black boots.

"One forty-five," Lauren replied.

Straightening up, she tucked a stray wisp of hair back into her braid, which she'd doubled under so it wouldn't flop. Then she put on her helmet. Butterflies had been going wild in her stomach all morning. She hoped she wouldn't throw up.

"All this for five minutes in the arena," she grumbled.

"Getting a little nervous?" Andie asked as she tightened Whisper's girth. The mare swished her tail and flattened her ears.

"I've been nervous all week," Lauren said. Standing on tiptoes, she stuck her rider number onto the brow band: 138. Maybe it was a lucky number.

"Lauren!" Mary Beth called as she and Jina hurried across the field to the van. Like Andie, they were wearing their Foxhall blazers. "Alicia just rode. She looked great."

"Mary Beth, her horse tried to throw her off," Jina said impatiently.

Mary Beth shrugged. "I thought that was one of those neat tricks dressage horses do."

"You mean a piaffe?" Lauren asked.

Andie snorted. "Honestly, Mary Beth, you are such a bonehead."

"What Andie means is, you only do a piaffe at the Grand Prix level," Lauren explained.

"Well, how was I supposed to know?" Mary Beth said huffily.

"I'd better get going," Lauren said. "Jina, will you give me a leg up?"

Putting two hands under Lauren's bent leg, Jina boosted her into the saddle.

Lauren looked down at her roommates. Andie checked the girth one last time, Mary Beth patted Whisper's neck, and Jina wiped a speck of mud from Lauren's boots.

"Well," Lauren said, finally, "I guess it's time. Here goes nothing."

"You'll do great," Jina said.

Lauren squeezed her calves against Whisper's sides, urging her forward.

"Good luck!" her roommates called.

Fifteen minutes later, Lauren walked Whisper around the perimeter of the competition arena. Inside the arena, the rider before her had given the final salute and was leaving the ring. At the far end, outside the arena at marker C, the judge sat behind a table under a canopy.

"Enter, salute, trot, track to the right," Lauren repeated under her breath. Her fingers tightened on the reins. Whisper quickened her pace, anticipating a signal.

Finally, the rider exited. Lauren shut her eyes tight. When the bell rang, she'd have ninety seconds to enter the ring.

Ninety seconds before she made a fool of herself in front of everyone.

Lauren snapped open her eyes. No. She had ninety seconds to do her best.

The bell rang, and Lauren's heart leaped to her throat.

This was it.

Whisper strode into the arena, her trot smooth, yet energetic. Lauren halted her at X. Neck arched, Whisper stood like a statue as Lauren held both reins in her left hand, crisply saluting the judge with her right.

A spasm of fear gripped Lauren as she signaled Whisper to trot again. But the mare took off, straight and even, turning right at C, her body correctly bending into the turn.

Wow, Lauren thought. *Whisper's going for it!* A shiver of excitement replaced some of the butterflies in her stomach.

Circle at B, Lauren recited silently, *then sit a trot and do a serpentine.*

But her body was already going through the movements. The hours of pretend riding in an imaginary arena had paid off. *Thanks, Ashley,*

Lauren thought. *Your idea works!*

Automatically, she sat deep, relaxing her seat bones in the saddle. At marker *C*, she shifted her left leg back, signaling for the canter. Whisper broke into a floating, balanced canter.

Lauren's spirits soared. She could have cantered all day. Almost too late, she remembered she needed to trot at *F*. Lauren closed her fingers on the reins, bringing Whisper smoothly back to a trot. Then, just before marker *K*, she asked Whisper to slow to a walk. The mare instantly responded.

Lauren sighed with relief. Halfway over! They were going to make it!

A few minutes later, Lauren finished her final salute. Applause broke out on the hillside above the arena. Jina, Mary Beth, Andie, Katherine, and the other Foxhall students were cheering loudly.

As Whisper strode back to *A*, Lauren patted her soundly on her sweaty neck.

"We did it!" Lauren told the mare excitedly. "We really did it!"

"Fifth place!" Mary Beth exclaimed proudly. She stood outside the suite, showing Lauren's pink ribbon to anyone who stuck her head into the hall. "My roommate placed fifth out of twenty riders!"

"Will you give me that!" Lauren screeched from the doorway. She charged into the hall, grabbing for the ribbon.

Laughing, Mary Beth held it over her head and ran down the hall, waving the ribbon.

"What's going on?" Jina asked, poking her head out of the suite.

"I'm going to kill Mary Beth if she doesn't give me that ribbon," Lauren growled. Then she burst out laughing. Mary Beth looked so silly, dancing down the hall in her poodle pajamas with the puffy sleeves.

"Mary Beth, throw it here!" Andie called. She dashed past Jina out of the suite, her arms raised like a football player about to catch a pass.

Lauren put her hands on her hips. "Knock it off, you guys."

Two girls from suite 4C came out and got into the game. Frustrated, Lauren darted from girl to girl, trying to catch the ribbon. Finally, Jina snatched it in midair and ran back into the suite.

Laughing and shouting, all the girls ran in

after her. Jina passed the ribbon to Lauren. But Andie dove in front of her, snatching it from Lauren's fingers.

"Touchdown!" Andie yelled as she belly-flopped on Mary Beth's bed.

Giggling, Lauren jumped on top of her.

"Pile up!" Mary Beth yelled, landing awkwardly on the heap.

"Lauren Remick!" someone hollered from the hall. "Phone call!"

"It must be my mom," Lauren said, struggling to get out of the tangle of girls. Barefoot, she ran into the hall and picked up the receiver.

"Mom?" she gasped, trying to catch her breath.

"Mom?" a voice exclaimed on the other end.

Lauren frowned. "Who is this?"

"Hello to you, too, Remick. How'd the dressage test go? Did you remember to serpentine from *A* to *C*?"

"Ashley?" Lauren asked, stunned.

"Who else?"

Lauren was so surprised, she didn't know what to say. "I um, um—" she sputtered nervously.

"Are you trying to say you weren't expecting me to call?" Ashley cut in.

Lauren cleared her throat. "Something like that."

"Well, I can understand *why*," Ashley said sharply. "It's too bad you can't see through the phone. They have me strapped to the bed with tubes and wires stuck everywhere. I told everyone it's just the flu, but the doctors keep insisting my body's so weak, I was about to catch pneumonia!"

"I'm so sorry, Ashley." Lauren gulped, blinking back the tears.

I won't cry, she told herself fiercely.

"Actually, I'm *not sorry* I did what I did," she said, her voice shaking.

There was a long pause. Lauren could hear Ashley breathing on the other end.

"I want you to get better," Lauren said softly. "And stronger. I want you to come back to Foxhall as soon as you're well."

There was more silence. Then Lauren heard a deep sigh.

"I know you thought you were doing the right thing," Ashley said finally. "And I guess everything will turn out okay. Dr. Stein says—"

"Dr. Stein?"

"Yeah. My parents called her. She specializes in teens with eating disorders."

Was Ashley finally admitting she had a problem? Lauren wondered.

"Anyway, Dr. Stein says as soon as I'm over the flu, I can go back to Foxhall," Ashley went on. "My parents and the school are insisting that I see her every day. That's a bummer, but the great thing is, I can show again in three weeks. I'll miss the next show, but Mrs. Caufield says I can still earn enough points to win the Junior Horse of the Year Award."

"That's terrific!" Lauren said.

"Well, don't get too excited. There is one more thing I have to say to you." Ashley's voice was stern.

Lauren braced herself for the worst.

"Congratulations!" Ashley sang out. "Lauren Remick, you passed the math midterm!"

"What?" Lauren almost fell on the floor.

"You *passed*. You got a C. You can stay in the riding program!"

"I did? I can?" Lauren couldn't believe her ears.

"Yup. Mr. Lyons called this morning. He thought maybe I should pass along the good news. You know, kind of as a way of patching things up."

Lauren let out her breath. She felt like a popped balloon, as if all the week's worries had whooshed out, leaving her flat.

"Wow," she said.

"You're welcome," Ashley said.

Lauren laughed. "Thank you! For *two* things." She told her about winning the fifth place ribbon.

"Way to go!" Ashley cheered. Then her voice lowered. "I've got to go now. Nurse Nasty is here with my evening snack—a high-protein milkshake. Yuck."

"'Bye, Ashley."

"'Bye." Abruptly, Ashley hung up and Lauren stared at the receiver. She still couldn't believe Ashley had called.

Squeals of laughter floated down the hall as Lauren slowly hung up the phone. Then she headed downstairs. She had one more thing to do before she could feel like partying.

Lauren knocked on the door of suite 3C. "Stephanie?"

Christina, Stephanie's roommate, opened the door. She had green goop all over her face.

"Hey, Stephanie," Christina called over her shoulder. "It's your kid sister."

Juniors only had to share the suite with one

roommate, so the girls' room looked enormous to Lauren. They each even had a closet of their own.

Stephanie sat cross-legged on her bed, painting her toenails. Her face was covered in green goop, too.

"Are you still my sister?" Lauren asked.

"Unfortunately," Stephanie said, without looking up.

"You'll have to excuse us. We're getting ready for big dates tomorrow," Christina told Lauren.

Lauren's eyes widened. "You are?"

"We wish," Stephanie said.

"So what do you want?" Stephanie asked.

Lauren glanced at Christina.

"I can take the hint." Christina held out both hands. "I need to wash this junk off my face anyway." She disappeared into the bathroom.

"So what's so important?" Stephanie asked, holding her foot in the air to inspect her new polish.

Lauren took a deep breath.

"I wanted to tell you that I think you were wrong when you told me I shouldn't have ratted on Ashley. And you were wrong to tell me

I should have minded my own business."

Startled, Stephanie looked up. A blob of polish dripped from the brush onto her foot.

"You think *I* was wrong?" Stephanie repeated, dabbing at the polish with a tissue.

Lauren flinched at her sister's sharp tone. But she nodded quickly. "Yes," she said, trying to sound confident. "Ashley needed help. It wasn't like I told because she snuck out on a date or forged a pass to the library."

Stephanie just stared at her. Lauren met her gaze.

Finally, Stephanie looked away.

"You might be right." Then she grinned at Lauren. "I said *might*. Now come on over and give me a hug."

Lauren sighed with relief. Crossing the room, she wrapped her arms around Stephanie's neck.

"Hey, you're smudging my face!" Stephanie complained.

Lauren pulled away and wiped the disgusting green glop off her own cheeks.

"'Bye, Steph," she said quickly, then turned and rushed outside to the hall.

She took the stairs two at a time. She couldn't wait to talk to her roommates.

They'd understood about math and Ashley and how worried she'd been. About *everything.*

Halfway down the hall, she heard loud voices coming from suite 4B. The door was closed. What was going on now?

Lauren stopped short.

Her roommates had taped her pink ribbon to the memo board. Under it they'd written:

> Won by Lauren Remick, a winner and a super roomie. You're the greatest!
>
> Andie, Jina, and Mary Beth

Tears filled Lauren's eyes. Hastily, she wiped them with the sleeve of her pajamas. Then beaming with happiness, she pushed open the door to suite 4B.

Don't miss the next book in the Riding Academy series: #5: MARY BETH'S HAUNTED RIDE

Andie stuck a piece of paper under Mary Beth's nose. "You dropped something, Finney."

It was the letter from Brad!

Mary Beth grabbed for it, but Andie jerked the paper away.

"Oooh. This must be real important if Finney wants it back so much." Grinning, Andie unfolded the letter.

Furious, Mary Beth snatched the paper from her roommate's grasp. "You're *not* reading my private letter from Brad."

Andie snorted. "Why would I want to read a dumb letter from some Hicksville nerd?"

Mary Beth stuck her nose in Andie's face. "You're just jealous because I have a boyfriend and you don't." With that, she yanked Dan's reins from Andie's hand and stomped away.

Maybe Brad wasn't exactly her boyfriend, Mary Beth admitted to herself. But he was a *boy,* and he was a *friend*. And he was coming to visit her.

That was more exciting than riding a dumb old horse any day.

ENTER TO WIN A RIDING ACADEMY T-SHIRT! 50 WINNERS!

Now you can join Mary Beth, Andie, Jina, and Lauren on their Riding Academy adventures with your very own Riding Academy T-Shirt. Just fill in the entry form below and return it by December 31, 1994. By random drawing we will select 50 winners, who will each receive a specially designed Riding Academy T-Shirt!

OFFICIAL RULES

1. No purchase necessary. To enter, complete the official entry form below or on a 3" x 5' plain piece of paper, print your name, complete address, date of birth, and the name of your favorite Riding Academy character. Mail your entry to: "Riding Academy Sweepstakes," P.O. Box 3857, Grand Central Station, New York, NY 10163. Enter as many times as you wish but mail each entry separately. Incomplete or incorrect entries are ineligible. No photocopies or mechanically reproduced entries will be accepted. Sweepstakes begins 7/1/94. All entries must be received by 12/31/94. Not responsible for lost, late, misdirected, damaged, incomplete, altered, illegible, or postage-due mail. Entries become the property of the sponsor and will not be returned.
2. Winners will be determined in random drawings no later than 1/31/95 by an independent judging organization whose decisions are final. All prizes are guaranteed to be awarded. Winners will be notified by mail. If any prize notification letter or any prize is returned to RANDOM HOUSE, INC. as undeliverable, the corresponding prize will be awarded to an alternate winner in a random drawing. No substitutions for prizes except as may be necessary due to unavailability, in which case a prize of equal or greater value will be awarded. Prizes are not transferable or redeemable for cash. No duplicate prizewinners. Prizes will be awarded within approximately 90 days after sweepstakes ends. Taxes are the responsibility of the winners. Acceptance of prize constitutes permission (except where prohibited by law) to use winners' names, hometowns, and likenesses for advertising, promotion, and publicity without additional compensation.
3. Prizes and estimated maximum retail value: (50) First Prizes: Riding Academy T-Shirt ($12.00 each).
4. Sweepstakes is open to legal residents of the United States and Canada (except void in the Province of Quebec) who, as of 1/31/95, are under 18 years of age. Odds of winning are determined by the total number of entries received. Distribution of this offer is estimated not to exceed 35,000. This sweepstakes is sponsored by RANDOM HOUSE, INC., 201 E. 50th Street, New York, NY 10022. Employees of RANDOM HOUSE, INC., its affiliates, subsidiaries, distributors, retailers, advertising and promotion agencies, and their immediate families are not eligible. All federal, state, and local rules and regulations apply. Void in Puerto Rico and where prohibited, taxed, or restricted by law.
5. For a list of prizewinners, send a self-addressed, stamped envelope before 12/31/94 to: "Riding Academy Winners," 201 East 50th Street, New York, NY 10022, ATT: Riding Academy Editor. Requests for the winners' names will be fulfilled after the sweepstakes drawing. DO NOT SEND ANY OTHER CORRESPONDENCE TO THIS ADDRESS.

Name ______________________ Date of Birth ____________

Street ______________________________________

City ______________________ State/Zip ____________

Where did you buy this Riding Academy book? ____________

❑ Bookstore ❑ Drugstore ❑ Supermarket ❑ Library ❑ Book Club ❑ Book Fair

❑ Other ______________________ (specify)

Who is your favorite Riding Academy character? ____________

VOLUME TEN

Jesus Speaks to His Apostles

Direction for Our Times
As given to Anne,
a lay apostle

VOLUME TEN

Direction for Our Times
As given to Anne, a lay apostle

ISBN-13: 978-0-9766841-9-0

Library of Congress Number: applied for

Publisher:
Direction for Our Times
9000 West 81st Street
Justice, IL 60458

708-496-9300
www.directionforourtimes.org

Direction for Our Times is a 501(c)(3) tax-exempt organization.

Manufactured in the United States of America

Graphic Design: Pete Massari

Painting of *Jesus Christ the Returning King* by Janusz Antosz

V0810

Direction for Our Times wishes to manifest its complete obedience and submission of mind and heart to the final and definitive judgment of the Magisterium of the Catholic Church and the local Ordinary regarding the supernatural character of the messages received by Anne, a lay apostle.

In this spirit, the messages of Anne, a lay apostle, have been submitted to her bishop, Most Reverend Leo O'Reilly, Bishop of Kilmore, Ireland, and to the Vatican Congregation for the Doctrine of the Faith for formal examination. In the meantime Bishop O'Reilly has given permission for their publication.

October 11, 2004

Dear Friends,

I am very much impressed with the messages delivered by Anne who states that they are received from God the Father, Jesus, and the Blessed Mother. They provide material for excellent and substantial meditation for those to whom they are intended, namely to the laity, to bishops and priests; and sinners with particular difficulties. These messages should not be read hurriedly but reserved for a time when heartfelt recollection and examination can be made.

I am impressed by the complete dedication of Anne to the authority of the magisterium, to her local Bishop and especially to the Holy Father. She is a very loyal daughter of the Church.

Sincerely in Christ,

Philip M. Hannan

Archbishop Philip M. Hannan, (Ret.)
President of FOCUS Worldwide Network
Retired Archbishop of New Orleans

PMH/aac

106 Metairie Lawn Dr. • Metairie, LA 70001 • Phone(504) 840-9898 • Fax(504) 840-9818

Dr. Mark I. Miravalle, S.T.D.
Professor of Theology and Mariology, Franciscan University of Steubenville
313 High Street • Hopedale, OH 43976 • U.S.A.
740-937-2277 • mmiravalle@franciscan.edu

Without in any way seeking to anticipate the final and definitive judgment of the local bishop and of the Holy See (to which we owe our filial obedience of mind and heart), I wish to manifest my personal discernment concerning the nature of the messages received by "Anne," a Lay Apostle.

After an examination of the reported messages and an interview with the visionary herself, I personally believe that the messages received by "Anne" are of supernatural origin.

The message contents are in conformity with the faith and morals teachings of the Catholic Church's Magisterium and in no way violate orthodox Catholic doctrine. The phenomena of the precise manner of how the messages are transmitted (i.e., the locutions and visions) are consistent with the Church's historical precedence for authentic private revelation. The spiritual fruits (cf. Mt. 7:17-20) of Christian faith, conversion, love, and interior peace, based particularly upon a renewed awareness of the indwelling Christ and prayer before the Blessed Sacrament, have been significantly manifested in various parts of the world within a relatively brief time since the messages have been received and promulgated. Hence the principal criteria used by ecclesiastical commissions to investigate reported supernatural events (message, phenomena, and spiritual fruits) are, in my opinion, substantially satisfied in the case of "Anne's" experience.

The messages which speak of the coming of Jesus Christ, the "Returning King" do not refer to an imminent end of the world with Christ's final physical coming, but rather call for a spiritual receptivity to an ongoing spiritual return of Jesus Christ, a dynamic advent of Jesus which ushers in a time of extraordinary grace and peace for humanity (in ways similar to the Fatima promise for an eventual era of peace as a result of the Triumph of the Immaculate Heart of Mary, or perhaps the "new springtime" for the Church referred to by the words of the great John Paul II).

As "Anne" has received permission from her local ordinary, Bishop Leo O'Reilly, for the spreading of her messages, and has also submitted all her writings to the Congregation for the Doctrine of the Faith, I would personally encourage, (as the Church herself permits), the prayerful reading of these messages, as they have constituted an authentic spiritual benefit for a significant number of Catholic leaders throughout the world.

Mark I. Miravalle

Dr. Mark Miravalle
Professor of Theology and Mariology
Franciscan University of Steubenville
October 13, 2006

Table of Contents

Introduction

Dear Reader,

I am a wife, mother of six, and a Secular Franciscan.

At the age of twenty, I was divorced for serious reasons and with pastoral support in this decision. In my mid-twenties I was a single parent, working and bringing up a daughter. As a daily Mass communicant, I saw my faith as sustaining and had begun a journey toward unity with Jesus, through the Secular Franciscan Order or Third Order.

My sister travelled to Medjugorje and came home on fire with the Holy Spirit. After hearing of her beautiful pilgrimage, I experienced an even more profound conversion. During the following year I experienced various levels of deepened prayer, including a dream of the Blessed Mother, where she asked me if I would work for Christ. During the dream she showed me that this special spiritual work would mean I would be separated from others in the world. She actually showed me my extended family and how I would be separated from them. I told her that I did not care. I would do anything asked of me.

Shortly after, I became sick with endometriosis. I have been sick ever since, with one thing or another. My sicknesses are always the types that mystify doctors in the beginning. This is part of the cross and I mention it because so many suffer in this way. I was told by my doctor that I would never conceive children. As a single parent, this did not concern me as I assumed it was God's will. Soon after, I met a wonderful man. My first marriage had been annulled and we married and conceived five children.

Spiritually speaking, I had many experiences that included what I now know to be interior locutions. These moments were beautiful and the words still stand out firmly in my heart, but I did not get excited because I was busy offering up illnesses and exhaustion. I took it as a matter of course that Jesus had to work hard to sustain me as He had given me a lot to handle. In looking back, I see that He was preparing me to do His work. My preparation period was long, difficult and not very exciting. From the outside, I think people thought, man, that woman has bad luck. From the inside, I saw that while my sufferings were painful and long lasting, my little family was growing in love, in size and in wisdom, in the sense that my husband and I certainly understood what was important and what was not important. Our continued crosses did that for us.

Various circumstances compelled my husband and me to move with our children far from my loved ones. I offered this up and must say it is the most difficult thing I have had to contend with. Living in exile brings many beautiful opportunities to align with Christ's will; however, you have to continually remind yourself that you are doing that. Otherwise you just feel sad. After several years in exile, I finally got the inspiration to go to Medjugorje. It was actually a gift from my husband for my fortieth birthday. I had tried to go once before, but circumstances prevented the trip and I understood it was not God's will. Finally, though, it was time and my eldest daughter and I found ourselves in front of St. James Church. It was her second trip to Medjugorje.

I did not expect or consider that I would experience anything out of the ordinary. My daughter, who loved it on her first trip, made many jokes about people looking for miracles. She affectionately calls Medjugorje a carnival for religious people. She also says it is the happiest place on earth. This young woman initially went there as a rebellious fourteen-year-old, who took the opportunity to travel abroad with her aunt. She returned calm and respectful, prompting my husband to say we would send all our teenagers on pilgrimage.

At any rate, we had a beautiful five days. I experienced a spiritual healing on the mountain. My daughter rested and prayed. A quiet but significant thing happened to me. During my Communions, I spoke with Jesus conversationally. I thought this was beautiful, but it had happened before on occasion so I was not stunned or overcome. I remember telling others that Communions in Medjugorje were powerful. I came home, deeply grateful to Our Lady for bringing us there.

The conversations continued all that winter. At some time in the six months that followed our trip, the conversations leaked into my life and came at odd times throughout the day. Jesus began to direct me with decision and I found it more and more difficult to refuse when He asked me to do this or that. I told no one.

During this time, I also began to experience direction from the Blessed Mother. Their voices are not hard to distinguish. I do not hear them in an auditory way, but in my soul or mind. By this time I knew that something remarkable was occurring and Jesus was telling me that He had special work for me, over and above my primary vocation as wife and mother. He told me to write the messages down and that He would arrange to have them published and disseminated. Looking back, it took Him a long time to get me comfortable enough where I was willing to trust Him. I trust His voice now and will continue to do my best to serve Him, given my constant struggle with weaknesses, faults, and the pull of the world.

Please pray for me as I continue to try to serve Jesus. Please answer "yes" to Him because He so badly needs us and He is so kind. He will take you right into His heart if you let Him. I am praying for you and am so grateful to God that He has given you these words. Anyone who knows Him must fall in love with Him, such is His goodness. If you have been struggling, this is your answer. He is coming to you in a special way through these words and the graces that flow through them.

Please do not fall into the trap of thinking that He cannot possibly mean for you to reach high levels of holiness. As I say somewhere in my writings, the greatest sign of the times is Jesus having to make do with the likes of me as His secretary. I consider myself the B-team, dear friends. Join me and together we will do our little bit for Him.

Message received from Jesus immediately following my writing of the above biographical information:

You see, My child, that you and I have been together for a long time. I was working quietly in your life for years before you began this work. Anne, how I love you. You can look back through your life and see so many "yes" answers to Me. Does that not please you and make you glad? You began to say "yes" to Me long before you experienced extraordinary graces. If you had not, My dearest, I could never have given you the graces or assigned this mission to you. Do you see how important it was that you got up every day, in your ordinary life, and said "yes" to your God, despite difficulty, temptation, and hardship? You

could not see the big plan as I saw it. You had to rely on your faith. Anne, I tell you today, it is still that way. You cannot see My plan, which is bigger than your human mind can accept. Please continue to rely on your faith as it brings Me such glory. Look at how much I have been able to do with you, simply because you made a quiet and humble decision for Me. Make another quiet and humble decision on this day and every day, saying, "I will serve God." Last night you served Me by bringing comfort to a soul in pain. You decided against yourself and for Me, through your service to him. There was gladness in heaven, Anne. You are Mine. I am yours. Stay with Me, My child. Stay with Me.

The Allegiance Prayer For All Lay Apostles

Dear God in heaven, I pledge my allegiance to You. I give You my life, my work and my heart. In turn, give me the grace of obeying Your every direction to the fullest possible extent. Amen.

September 23, 2004
Jesus

Dear children, I dedicate this little Volume to My servants, those who seek to spread My message of love and salvation. Dearest souls, so bravely serving the Kingdom, your reward will be great. Many of you have been pulled from sin and darkness yourselves and brought to the light. I welcomed your return as if you were My only child. The place reserved for you in My heart felt complete when you came back to Me. Truly and completely do I love you.

Now, we must seek out others. You will find them everywhere, and this is why you are serving everywhere. The souls who are at risk of eternal separation from Me are in each area of the worldly domain. Some are poor, some are wealthy. Some are looked down upon and some are highly respected. Some claim goodness, and some do not hide their affinity with the enemy. Regardless, I want them all. In this Volume, I intend to instruct you on how to reclaim what is ours, the souls of our brothers and sisters.

The first strategy for bringing others to heaven is setting an example of joy in service. Yes, many of you are being asked to suffer for Me and I thank you. Remember that if you are suffering, you must always unite your grief and pain to My grief and pain. You must say, I suffer because My Jesus is suffering. So be it. I will accept your "yes" and use it powerfully for necessary redemptive graces. You are cooperating with Me and your cooperation with Me is helping Me to save souls. Rest in that because it is truth. You must begin to equate even your smallest crosses to so many souls rescued from darkness. Children, I know you are limited by your earthly vision. I understand. But this is the time to believe with dedication. We agreed, you and I, that if you made a decision for Me, you would serve, regardless of your feelings on any given day. One way to serve is to offer your little sufferings to Me continually. Again I say to you, suffering saves souls. Be at peace in these crosses, united to My cross, and set the example of joy in service. This is the first way we will draw souls from the darkness.

September 24, 2004
Jesus

I do not spare My friends, it is true. If you are My friend, you will know suffering. Through your sufferings, you will know Me. I will visit you with grief perhaps. I may visit you with hardships and trying situations. Perhaps you will know Me in sickness or emotional difficulties. If you are My friend, you will know suffering. So why do I do this? Why do I allow My dear servants pain and suffering when truly I am the all-powerful God who can literally abduct the wind if I choose? My dearest little slaves, I am the King, but My Kingdom is not of this world. This world belongs to Me, of course, and I am ultimately in control of it, as you will see in your future. But you would not give an infant a book on the divinity of Christ. It would be meaningless to that infant. First, you must teach that infant to read. Before that, you must nurture the infant with physical nourishment and a great deal of love. Only then will the infant become predisposed to cooperate with the learning process that must occur to learn to read.

There is indeed a great deal that must occur before a subject of My Kingdom can study the divinity of Christ. Let me give you another example. The infant, as he is learning to walk, often looks up to his mother and says, "Carry me." Often you will hear a mother say, "No, my little one. I prefer that you walk." Could the mother lift the child into her arms? Of course she could. What reason could a mother have for allowing her child to walk? Is the case not often that the wise mother wishes her child to learn to walk properly, and then to run? To do so, this mother understands that her child needs to exercise the muscles needed to complete these acts. Well, I am like the wise mother. I understand that in order for My friends to experience divinity and the life of the divine to the fullest, they must learn by exercising their spiritual muscles. The more you do so, the more you will experience in heaven. You are not competing with each other; you are learning to love Me. You are each created to love Me in a different way and those lessons are learned each day in your trials and challenges. Like the wise mother, I do not leave you toddling along by yourself when you are unsteady. I will never leave you. But you must learn. Do not begrudge Me your sufferings, little

souls. You cannot begin to imagine their value.

September 25, 2004
Jesus

My little serving souls feel the weakness of their bodies. Your bodies often tell you that you should rest, and yet, you see that I have additional work for you. Brothers and sisters in the vineyards of the world, you will reap the harvest with a steady pace. If you are feeling hurried, you must remember, something is amiss. You will occasionally feel the pressure to complete a given task, of course, but generally speaking you should exert a steady and constant effort in My service. Do not be like worldly souls who exhibit a burst of service, and then fall away from Me. This is not helpful. Heaven relies most heavily on those who are consistent. So while I do not want you to pamper your body or treat it like a god, you should be respectful of its needs because it houses your soul and through it I am achieving the most miraculous things. When you find yourself listening to a stranger and providing solace or heavenly witness, you must consider that I am at work. Without your cooperation, without your body, I could not be there in the way that the soul needed to see Me. Through

you I become physically present. Care for your body. Do not idolize it.

September 27, 2004
Jesus

My servants often have difficulty overcoming their self-will. Brothers and sisters, self-will does not lead to Me. Self-will leads away from Me. That concept is very simple. You may hear souls saying, "What is His will? Help me to know His will." Well, truly, if I am asked, I will answer. Your Jesus, who calls you so firmly into service right now, will not leave you wondering. Be certain you are asking Me to show you My will in the silence of contemplation. There are times when souls know My will but find it repugnant. You must know that I understand this revulsion for the self-sacrificing that often accompanies My will. But children of the all-powerful God, know that this offering of your will can make you a saint quite quickly. I did not want to suffer great torture and pain in My body. Believe Me when I say that I shuddered in contemplation of the cross. Yet, the cross was the Father's will for Me. So be it. I shouldered My cross in humility and obedience and through the cross I redeemed you. You are worth the sacrifice. And it was temporary. The sacri-

fices you are being asked to make are also temporary. You are not and will not be asked to relinquish anything for eternity. Your eternity, based on the beautiful merits of your sacrifices and service, will be filled with joy and reward. So you, like Me, are being asked to carry this cross or that cross, make this sacrifice or that sacrifice, for a short time, so that I, through your obedience and cooperation, can bring other souls to heaven.

Consider how important each soul is to Me. Consider Me, Jesus, in the form of My humanity. As I suffered anguish in the Garden, I was tempted with every form of temptation. Let us say that the enemy offered Me every soul on earth, but one. For stepping away from the chance of saving this one soul, I could escape the cross. Add to the consideration that this one soul might reject Me and be lost anyway. Would I be tempted? Would you?

Now consider that this one soul was yours.

What do you think I would say?

I assure you, My beloved, I said NO.

Do not hold back from Me, little servants. Do not sidestep the divine will. Your family needs you and I need you.

September 28, 2004
Jesus

Dear souls of the Kingdom, you are called to service. You know this. You have heard My call and rested in My anguish. I want to talk to you about your duty. Perhaps you hear My call and feel resistance at what it is I am asking from you. Let me promise you that you will be given exactly what you need to embrace your portion of this mission. Do not be afraid to stand beside Me as I move into the world through each one of you. Souls will see you with their physical eyes, but they will experience Me. Your fears, your hesitance, have no bearing on how you will perform for Me. Do not worry about your ability when it comes to completing your duty. Do not worry about your lack of strength. It will come from Me. It will flow deeply and completely from Me. Your willingness to serve is all that is required.

September 29, 2004
Jesus

My dearest little serving souls, how I love you. You serve so diligently and do not realize at all how grateful is your Jesus. My gratitude could flow over you in such a way that you would experience it in your humanity. But if that were to happen, the merit from your service might be decreased. So I keep that to Myself and place it in the most special place in heaven, your place. It will be here waiting for you when you arrive. All of your crosses, each one, obtain merit for your soul and salvation for others. The more unpleasant the cross, the more merit and salvation obtained. You do not see Me, but you believe in Me. I do not speak these words to you, but you know that these are My words. Children, I am working silently in your beautiful souls all through each day, all through each night. The gratitude is there in My presence. The gratitude is there in your peace. The gratitude is there in the quietness of your soul. You are not restless and unhappy like souls wandering without Me. You are learning not to harbor unnecessary fears. If you allow Me, I will eradicate all fear for you. I care for your interests. I care for your families. You are My disciples, My apostles. I cared lovingly for My first twelve and I care just as lovingly for each one of you. Do not think that your Jesus is not grateful, simply because I am quiet. I thank you for the smallest act and the largest crosses. You will have a glorious eternity, little soldiers. Believe this, as it is truth.

September 30, 2004
Jesus

From now on, I will think of you as My apostles. As I prepared My original apostles to begin My beautiful Church on earth, I now commission you to reclaim My beautiful Church. You have such great heavenly assistance. When I speak of My Church, I am speaking of the body of the Church, comprised of its people. You are to call them back to the safety of the family of God. I send you out as I sent out the first group. You are to speak freely of Me. If a soul rejects Me, hold no malice for that soul. Simply pray for him and move along, seeking out another. Often you are like a farmer sowing seeds. I, Myself, must reap the harvest. This should not concern you because to insist on reaping what you have sown in this instance is not appropriate. Sometimes God is needed to ignite the divine. Use My words, dear little apostles. Spread them everywhere. Keep your words limited and allow Me to claim the soul. You will soften the soul by loving the person. Your love and your example can predispose a soul so that I can find the opening I need. What joy is there in this work! How satisfying is a rescue mission when souls are saved. And they will be saved, do not fear. You will be successful, but only I can measure your success. You are successful now, are you not? You are following My will. You are working for the Kingdom. You are preparing to go out into the world on the greatest work of mercy ever known to your world. Children, dear apostles, there is great kinship between you. Support each other and encourage each other. Do not judge, but neither withhold heavenly obtained wisdom if a fellow apostle is in error. I am your guide. Ask Me if I want you to correct someone. All is well. We begin.

October 1, 2004
Jesus

My little apostles must climb steadily up the steep hill to heaven. By doing this, moving steadily, you bring many souls behind you. If you leave the path to examine this distraction or that earthly offering, you will lose souls. This is a time for sustained service. You have experience and your experience tells you that service to the Lord is not glamorous. On the contrary, service to Me is often quite dreary in appearance, when compared to what the children of the world are doing. While others amuse themselves, My servants are working. Well, dear ones, I do not want you to be downhearted, so at this time, I am going to give graces for My apostles to have the greatest joy in their service to Me. Remember that others must be drawn home to their family. To do that, We must make them see that the household of God is a good and joyful place to dwell. So in each day, in each little service to the Kingdom, you must accept My joy. If you begin to feel downhearted, you must come quickly to My Sacred Heart or to the Immaculate Heart of our Mother. We will replace your gloom with joy again so that others will be drawn. We are a family of happiness and peace. We are calm and confident. We know that God is good and that He is our Father who will not let us perish. Why, dear apostles, would we be sad? If you lose worldly possessions, understand that you have sent them here to heaven and you will collect them when you arrive. You will collect vastly greater things in heaven than you have given to Me on earth because I am all generosity. So let nothing grieve you. Nothing.

October 2, 2004
Jesus

My little servants must follow their mother. Our beautiful mother, Mary, has been given the greatest power during this time. This is My time but this is also Mary's time. Her power comes to her directly from the throne of God. Children, when you are concerned about the many misleading powers in your world today, ask this simple question. "Does the power for the alleged claim come from God the Father who sent His only Son into the world?" If the answer is no, then the power is being obtained from the enemy. Does this sound confusing to you? It should not sound confusing, because it is clear. If you are still confused, it is because you do not want to relinquish some habit that has gotten hold of you. Be vigilant here, brothers and sisters. There are impostors everywhere and the impostors do not seek the good of your soul. The enemy, in the form of these powers, seeks the destruction of anything that is holy in you. The enemy seeks your soul. The Holy Spirit within you will object and warn you if you have been nourishing the Holy Spirit. Do not become involved with anything that reminds you of fortune telling or healing. These habits are sinful. You will be held accountable. Speak out against them, warning your brothers and sisters. Christians in the world have become easy targets of the enemy's followers because they are lukewarm. Not My little apostles, though. You will know the truth and speak it loudly. Warn others, please. We are losing souls in this manner.

October 4, 2004
Jesus

My dear little apostles know great weariness. Be comfortable with your fatigue. See it as a sign that you are laboring for the Kingdom. Nothing more, nothing less. Do not allow the enemy to persuade you that weariness is a sign that you should stop working with Me. I understand weariness and I understand human discouragement. You might say that one feeds the other. I have spoken to you in the past about your bodies. Little apostles, I want you to get enough rest. By this, I want to state clearly that I refer to sleeping at night. I do not mean extended holidays from your duties. My apostles and saints throughout the ages always tried to live moderately in all things. In this way their bodies were treated with respect and could serve. You are children of God and you are true servants in a time when I have many enemies, few friends, and the greatest work to do. So heed My words and if you are having trouble in the area of moderation, seek the help of your brothers and sisters who have gone before you. I am your beloved Jesus. I love you most tenderly.

I will guide you in this area, as in every area of your time of service.

October 5, 2004
Jesus

I speak to you, My true servants. How I rely on you all. Each of you has a divine purpose and a role in the coming of My Kingdom. Each of you has a certain number of souls who can be brought back to My loving heart through your service. If you say "yes" to Me, I will use you. You are experienced and know this. But what I want to remind you of today is this. If you say "yes" to Me, and allow Me to minister to your world through you, you yourself will move closer and closer to My Sacred Heart. Deeply into My heart will I draw you. Deeply into the divine mysteries will you be brought. Little apostles, your mission involves your movement to Me. Your holiness and your spiritual growth are linked to the fulfilment of My mission for you. So yes, I need your service. Yes, you bear a certain amount of responsibility. But the benefit is all to you. You will find your salvation in your mission.

October 6, 2004
Jesus

My dear apostles, how hard you work for your Jesus. How beautifully I am able to flow through you. You will witness many conversions through your service to Me during this time because I am sending a great flood of graces into the world. Souls will return to Me and then they, too, will join the rescue mission. We will grow in number and in strength. All renewals begin this way, and initially rest upon the courage of a few. I am pleased. Our mother is also pleased because she is finding hearts open to her love and her service. Remain always close to her Immaculate Heart and she will sustain you, even in the most difficult situations. Difficulties will come, My dear ones. You understand that the work you do for heaven is destined to save many. As such, you will draw resistance, but it will not impact the work so you may be at peace. This mission is divine in origin and none will stand successfully against it.

October 7, 2004
Jesus

My little apostles must put aside tasks that do not further My will. At this time, I am asking each one of you to bring the Good News to souls. This is your heavenly instruction. I ask that you do this through your duty, first of all, because it is in living the holy and sacred life, following Me in your daily duty, that I can bring you to holiness. This example of faithfulness will say far more to others than if you neglected your duty. So that is your first priority and you may rest in the fact that this comes from Me. The second priority, then, must be the spread of these words. I want My words to move through your world steadily. I do not want a frantic haste, but neither do I want unnecessary delay. If you ask Me to show you your role in this mission, I will show you. You must say "yes" to Me. I speak to your hearts, little apostles. You know Me because you follow Me. Now is the time to let nothing distract you from the path to heaven. On that path you will find that I am asking you to bring this mission to fruition. This is the time for which you have been prepared. Many join the cause. Welcome them. Move forward with the greatest

humility because you have each been chosen to do your little part. With your beautiful and total "yes" I intend to save many souls. Do not be distracted. If you find you have been called, answer Me with love and you will find yourself immersed in heavenly grace.

October 8, 2004
Jesus

Little servants, seek only the divine will. On each day I want you to consider what I require from you. This means you will often find yourself realigning your activities to fit into My needs. Your time must be fruitful for the Kingdom and for that to occur, you must always ask Me what I would like you to do with your time. You see that I wish there to be constant communication between us. This may seem like a burden to you at first, but you will quickly become comfortable with unity to heaven. If heaven is to flow through you into the world, and that is the goal, you must let heaven direct everything. You know that we in heaven are willing to do that for you. We know that you are striving to allow heaven to direct you. So all that is needed is practice. How often we have asked you to practice. You are coming along, little apostles, and you are witnessing the way it is to be, with you serving and Me directing. Move forward daily, always forward, in My service, and you will see souls returning. I am with you in everything.

October 9, 2004
Jesus

My dear little apostles must heed My words in all calm. I am sending you the clearest instructions so that you have a clear vision of your mission. We are pulling souls back into the safety of the Christian family. We do so with love. My dear ones, I love you. I call you into service in all love and through your service to Me you will gain the greatest of graces for the intentions you hold dear. Do not fear that you will lose by your service to the Kingdom. There is only gain possible for you. Give Me each of your concerns and begin. Walk each day in the knowledge that you are fulfilling God's holy will for you and fulfilling your role in the Kingdom. It is for this mission you were placed on earth at this time. Do not refuse Me. Say "yes" to Jesus. You will be filled with My light. Step forward in faith and allow My divine understanding to come to you.

October 11, 2004
Jesus

My dear little apostles, I will always be with you. You walk in the world and My graces flow out from you. Because I confirm you in the light, you spread heavenly light wherever you go. During this time you will begin to see this more clearly. This is a result of the vast amount of grace that is flowing through each one of you into your world. There will be those who will say that Christ's followers have always done this for the world. This is true, of course. But do not believe that these times are like other times. These times are different for many reasons. I am returning. The process has begun. Let none of My followers deny that I am working with a profound urgency. Despite the need for this urgency, I am also spreading a profound sense of calm and peace. All is well, little apostles. You have chosen wisely and you will serve heaven in all peace and trust.

October 13, 2004
Jesus

I want My apostles to understand that I am always seeking new souls to join us. This group of workers who labor for souls must increase. We must pull as many as possible into the field of labor. In this way we will bring many back into the safety of My Sacred Heart. How joyful is the service to heaven. Contemplate this fact often, dear servants. You are laboring hard, it is true, but not without success. My words and graces flow so powerfully into your world. All cynicism, all hatred, cannot stand before My words. My words flow over cynicism and hatred and destroy these symptoms of darkness. Souls want to believe in Me. Souls want to trust Me. You are giving them the opportunity to do so by your example and by your life of service. My dearest little workers, how you delight Me. Truly, My just anger is abated by your humility and willingness. Do not be downhearted at the burdens you carry. You carry them for the Kingdom and each burden will win souls. Each soul is as precious as your soul. This should help you to understand My determination. I send you

great courage today to sustain you in your mission.

October 14, 2004
Jesus

This work is of the greatest of importance because through these words I give encouragement to My little apostles who work so diligently for the Kingdom. Dear servants of the Returning King, you will not be sorry you sacrificed for Me. During the whole of your eternity you will reap the rewards for having done so. In a time when few understand the concept of sacrifice, you are giving of yourselves, day after day, to bring about My goals. You are serving Me and you are serving your fellow man. How many can say that during these days? In the days to come, more and more will be alerted to the cause. There will be those who will say no to Me. When this occurs, you will simply continue to press forward with the work. Do not even pause, dear apostles, because this is to be expected. Simply rededicate yourself and continue, understanding that it is those very souls we work to bring salvation to.

It can be a bitter job at times, walking with Me, but only if you pause too long. If you are moving always closer to Me, you will not become bitter. I send only peace and love. Bitterness comes from sharing the view of those who serve the enemy. I do not advise this, of course, except for the briefest moment to determine why it is that you serve the light. Service to Me brings all that is good and holy. You will know My service by the fruits that come from Me and you will identify unity with Me by the peace in your soul. When you are fearful, you must come to Me for fresh courage. It will be yours in any amount necessary to accomplish this work. All that I have is yours. All that you need is yours. All of heaven, dear apostles, will be yours.

October 15, 2004
Jesus

My apostles of the light walk in the greatest of grace. My heavenly grace surrounds you at all times. You have heaven with you and heaven will assist you in everything. The work you do for this mission will truly seem effortless on your part because while we in heaven are flowing it through you, it does not come from you. So you see that a commitment to this mission of mercy will mean that you serve Me, but you are serving Me anyway. You will not find that you are working more strenuously in the spreading of these words than you would have otherwise because so much of what you do will be blessed by the most profound gifts of grace. When you allow Me to flow through you, I do most of the work. You are merely the cooperative vessels. Dear souls, come to Me often for sustenance. Confess your sins and remain filled with heavenly graces. I will never leave you and together we will do the greatest things for the Kingdom.

Appendix

The Lay Apostolate of Jesus Christ the Returning King

We seek to be united to Jesus in our daily work, and through our vocations, in order to obtain graces for the conversion of sinners. Through our cooperation with the Holy Spirit, we will allow Jesus to flow through us to the world, bringing His light. We do this in union with Mary, our Blessed Mother, with the Communion of Saints, with all of God's holy angels, and with our fellow lay apostles in the world.

Guidelines for Lay Apostles

As lay apostles of Jesus Christ the Returning King, we agree to perform our basic obligations as practicing Catholics. Additionally, we will adopt the following spiritual practices, as best we can:

1. **Allegiance Prayer** and **Morning Offering**, plus a brief prayer for the Holy Father
2. **Eucharistic Adoration**, one hour per week
3. **Prayer Group Participation**, monthly, at which we pray the Luminous Mysteries of the Holy Rosary and read the Monthly Message
4. **Monthly Confession**
5. Further, we will follow the example of Jesus Christ as set out in the Holy Scripture, treating all others with His patience and kindness.

Allegiance Prayer

Dear God in heaven, I pledge my allegiance to You. I give You my life, my work and my heart. In turn, give me the grace of obeying Your every direction to the fullest possible extent. Amen.

Morning Offering

O Jesus, through the Immaculate Heart of Mary, I offer You the prayers, works, joys and sufferings of this day, for all the intentions of Your Sacred Heart, in union with the Holy Sacrifice of the Mass throughout the world, in reparation for my sins, and for the intentions of the Holy Father. Amen.

Prayer for the Holy Father

Blessed Mother of Jesus, protect our Holy Father, Benedict XVI, and bless his intentions.

Five Luminous Mysteries

1. The Baptism of Jesus
2. The Wedding at Cana
3. The Proclamation of the Kingdom of God
4. The Transfiguration
5. The Institution of the Eucharist

Promise from Jesus to His Lay Apostles

May 12, 2005

Your message to souls remains constant. Welcome each soul to the rescue mission. You may assure each lay apostle that just as they concern themselves with My interests, I will concern Myself with theirs. They will be placed in My Sacred Heart and I will defend and protect them. I will also pursue complete conversion of each of their loved ones. So you see, the souls who serve in this rescue mission as My beloved lay apostles will know peace. The world cannot make this promise as only heaven can bestow peace on a soul. This is truly heaven's mission and I call every one of heaven's children to assist Me. You will be well rewarded, My dear ones.

Prayers taken from The Volumes

Prayers to God the Father

"What can I do for my Father in heaven?"

"I trust You, God. I offer You my pain in the spirit of acceptance and I will serve You in every circumstance."

"God my Father in heaven, You are all mercy. You love me and see my every sin. God, I call on You now as the Merciful Father. Forgive my every sin. Wash away the stains on my soul so that I may once again rest in complete innocence. I trust You, Father in heaven. I rely on You. I thank You. Amen."

"God my Father, calm my spirit and direct my path."

"God, I have made mistakes. I am sorry. I am Your child, though, and seek to be united to You."

"I believe in God. I believe Jesus is calling me. I believe my Blessed Mother has requested my help. Therefore I am going to pray on this day and every day."

"God my Father, help me to understand."

Prayers to Jesus

"Jesus, I give You my day."

"Jesus, how do You want to use me on this day? You have a willing servant in me, Jesus. Allow me to work for the Kingdom."

"Lord, what can I do today to prepare for Your coming? Direct me, Lord, and I will see to Your wishes."

"Lord, help me."

"Jesus, love me."

Prayers to the Angels

"Angels from heaven, direct my path."

"Dearest angel guardian, I desire to serve Jesus by remaining at peace. Please obtain for me the graces necessary to maintain His divine peace in my heart."

Prayers for a Struggling Soul

"Jesus, what do You think of all this? Jesus, what do You want me to do for this soul? Jesus, show me how to bring You into this situation."

"Angel guardian, thank you for your constant vigil over this soul. Saints in heaven, please assist this dear angel."

Prayers for Children

"God in heaven, You are the Creator of all things. Please send Your graces down upon our world."

"Jesus, I love You."

"Jesus, I trust in You. Jesus, I trust in You. Jesus, I trust in You."

"Jesus, I offer You my day."

"Mother Mary, help me to be good."

How to Recite the Chaplet of Divine Mercy

The Chaplet of Mercy is recited using ordinary Rosary beads of five decades. The Chaplet is preceded by two opening prayers from the *Diary* of Saint Faustina and followed by a closing prayer.

1. Make the Sign of the Cross

In the name of the Father, and of the Son, and of the Holy Spirit. Amen.

2. Optional Opening Prayers

You expired, Jesus, but the source of life gushed forth for souls, and the ocean of mercy opened up for the whole world. O Fount of Life, unfathomable Divine Mercy, envelop the whole world and empty Yourself out upon us.

O Blood and Water, which gushed forth from the Heart of Jesus as a fountain of mercy for us, I trust in You!

3. Our Father

Our Father, who art in heaven, hallowed be Thy name. Thy Kingdom come. Thy will be done on earth as it is in heaven. Give us this day our daily bread. And forgive us our trespasses, as we forgive those who trespass against us. And lead us not into temptation, but deliver us from evil. Amen.

4. Hail Mary

Hail Mary, full of grace, the Lord is with thee. Blessed art thou among women, and blessed is the fruit of thy womb, Jesus. Holy Mary, Mother of God, pray for us sinners, now and at the hour of our death. Amen.

5. The Apostles' Creed

I believe in God, the Father Almighty, Creator of heaven and earth. I believe in Jesus Christ, His only Son, our Lord. He was conceived by the power of the Holy Spirit and born of the Virgin Mary. He suffered under Pontius Pilate, was crucified, died, and was buried. He descended to the dead. On the third day He rose again. He ascended into heaven, and is seated at the right hand of the Father. He will come again to judge the living and the dead. I believe in the Holy Spirit, the holy Catholic Church, the Communion of Saints, the forgiveness of sins, the resurrection of the body, and life everlasting. Amen.

6. The Eternal Father

Eternal Father, I offer You the Body and Blood, Soul and Divinity of Your dearly beloved Son, our Lord, Jesus Christ, in atonement for our sins and those of the whole world.

7. On the Ten Small Beads of Each Decade

For the sake of His Sorrowful Passion, have mercy on us and on the whole world.

8. Repeat for the remaining decades

Saying the "Eternal Father" (6) on the "Our Father" bead and then 10 "For the sake of His Sorrowful Passion" (7) on the following "Hail Mary" beads.

9. Conclude with Holy God

Holy God, Holy Mighty One, Holy Immortal One, have mercy on us and on the whole world.

10. Optional Closing Prayer

Eternal God, in whom mercy is endless and the treasury of compassion inexhaustible, look kindly upon us and increase Your mercy in us, that in difficult moments we might not despair nor become despondent, but with great confidence submit ourselves to Your holy will, which is Love and Mercy itself.

To learn more about the image of The Divine Mercy, the Chaplet of Divine Mercy and the series of revelations given to St. Faustina Kowalska please contact:

Marians of the Immaculate Conception
Stockbridge, Massachusetts 01263
Telephone 800-462-7426
www.marian.org

How to Pray the Rosary

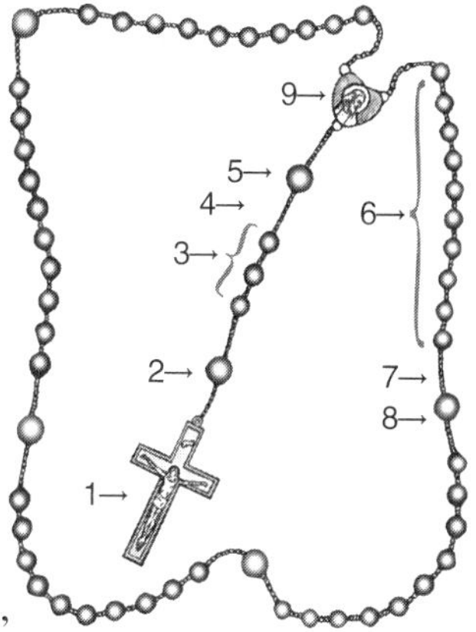

1. Make the Sign of the Cross and say the "Apostles Creed."
2. Say the "Our Father."
3. Say three "Hail Marys."
4. Say the "Glory be to the Father."
5. Announce the First Mystery; then say the "Our Father."
6. Say ten "Hail Marys," while meditating on the Mystery.
7. Say the "Glory be to the Father." After each decade say the following prayer requested by the Blessed Virgin Mary at Fatima: "O my Jesus, forgive us our sins, save us from the fires of hell, lead all souls to Heaven, especially those in most need of Thy mercy."
8. Announce the Second Mystery: then say the "Our Father." Repeat 6 and 7 and continue with the Third, Fourth, and Fifth Mysteries in the same manner.
9. Say the "Hail, Holy Queen" on the medal after the five decades are completed.

As a general rule, depending on the season, the Joyful Mysteries are said on Monday and Saturday; the Sorrowful Mysteries on Tuesday and Friday;

the Glorious Mysteries on Wednesday and Sunday; and the Luminous Mysteries on Thursday.

Papal Reflections of the Mysteries

The Joyful Mysteries

The Joyful Mysteries are marked by the joy radiating from the event of the Incarnation. This is clear from the very first mystery, the Annunciation, where Gabriel's greeting to the Virgin of Nazareth is linked to an invitation to messianic joy: "Rejoice, Mary." The whole of salvation… had led up to this greeting. (Prayed on Mondays and Saturdays, and optional on Sundays during Advent and the Christmas Season.)

The Luminous Mysteries

Moving on from the infancy and the hidden life in Nazareth to the public life of Jesus, our contemplation brings us to those mysteries which may be called in a special way "Mysteries of Light." Certainly, the whole mystery of Christ is a mystery of light. He is the "Light of the world" (John 8:12). Yet this truth emerges in a special way during the years of His public life. (Prayed on Thursdays.)

The Sorrowful Mysteries

The Gospels give great prominence to the Sorrowful Mysteries of Christ. From the beginning, Christian piety, especially during the Lenten devotion of the Way of the Cross, has focused on the individual moments of the Passion, realizing that here is found the culmination of the revelation of God's love and the source of our salvation. (Prayed on Tuesdays and Fridays, and optional on Sundays during Lent.)

The Glorious Mysteries

"The contemplation of Christ's face cannot stop at the image of the Crucified One. He is the Risen One!" The Rosary has always expressed this knowledge born of faith and invited the believer to pass beyond the darkness of the Passion in order to gaze upon Christ's glory in the Resurrection and Ascension… Mary herself would be raised to that same glory in the Assumption. (Prayed on Wednesdays and Sundays.)

From the *Apostolic Letter The Rosary of the Virgin Mary*, Pope John Paul II, Oct. 16, 2002.

Prayers of the Rosary

The Sign of the Cross

In the name of the Father, and of the Son, and of the Holy Spirit. Amen.

The Apostles' Creed

I believe in God, the Father Almighty, Creator of heaven and earth. I believe in Jesus Christ, His only Son, our Lord. He was conceived by the power of the Holy Spirit and born of the Virgin Mary. He suffered under Pontius Pilate, was crucified, died, and was buried. He descended to the dead. On the third day He rose again. He ascended into heaven, and is seated at the right hand of the Father. He will come again to judge the living and the dead. I believe in the Holy Spirit, the holy Catholic Church, the Communion of Saints, the forgiveness of sins, the resurrection of the body, and life everlasting. Amen.

Our Father

Our Father, who art in heaven, hallowed be Thy name. Thy Kingdom come. Thy will be done on earth as it is in heaven. Give us this day our daily bread. And forgive us our trespasses, as we forgive those who trespass against us. And lead us not into temptation, but deliver us from evil. Amen.

Hail Mary

Hail Mary, full of grace, the Lord is with thee. Blessed art thou among women, and blessed is the fruit of thy womb, Jesus. Holy Mary, Mother of God, pray for us sinners, now and at the hour of our death. Amen.

Glory Be to the Father

Glory be to the Father, and to the Son, and to the Holy Spirit. As it was in the beginning, is now, and ever shall be, world without end. Amen.

Hail Holy Queen

Hail, Holy Queen, Mother of Mercy, our life, our sweetness and our hope. To thee do we cry, poor banished children of Eve. To thee do we send up our sighs, mourning and weeping in this valley of tears. Turn then, most gracious Advocate, thine eyes of mercy towards us. And after this, our exile, show unto us the blessed fruit of thy womb, Jesus. O clement, O loving, O sweet Virgin Mary!

Pray for us, O Holy Mother of God.
That we may be made worthy of the promises of Christ.

The Mysteries

First Joyful Mystery: The Annunciation

And when the angel had come to her, he said, "Hail, full of grace, the Lord is with thee. Blessed art thou among women." (*Luke* 1:28)

One *Our Father*, Ten *Hail Marys*,
One *Glory Be*, etc.

Fruit of the Mystery: ***Humility***

Second Joyful Mystery: The Visitation

Elizabeth was filled with the Holy Spirit and cried out in a loud voice: "Blest are you among women and blest is the fruit of your womb."(*Luke* 1:41-42)

One *Our Father*, Ten *Hail Marys*,
One *Glory Be*, etc.

Fruit of the Mystery: ***Love of Neighbor***

Third Joyful Mystery: The Birth of Jesus

She gave birth to her first-born Son and wrapped Him in swaddling clothes and laid Him in a manger, because there was no room for them in the place where travelers lodged. (*Luke* 2:7)

One *Our Father*, Ten *Hail Marys*,
One *Glory Be*, etc.

Fruit of the Mystery: ***Poverty***

Fourth Joyful Mystery: The Presentation

When the day came to purify them according to the law of Moses, the couple brought Him up to Jerusalem so that He could be presented to the Lord, for it is written in the law of the Lord, "Every first-born male shall be consecrated to the Lord."

(*Luke* 2:22-23)

One *Our Father*, Ten *Hail Marys*,
One *Glory Be*, etc.

Fruit of the Mystery: ***Obedience***

Fifth Joyful Mystery: The Finding of the Child Jesus in the Temple

On the third day they came upon Him in the temple sitting in the midst of the teachers, listening to them and asking them questions. (*Luke* 2:46)

One *Our Father*, Ten *Hail Marys*,
One *Glory Be*, etc.

Fruit of the Mystery: ***Joy in Finding Jesus***

First Luminous Mystery: The Baptism of Jesus

And when Jesus was baptized… the heavens were opened and He saw the Spirit of God descending like a dove, and alighting on Him, and lo, a voice from heaven, saying "this is My beloved Son," with whom I am well pleased." (*Matthew* 3:16-17)

One *Our Father*, Ten *Hail Marys*,
One *Glory Be*, etc.

Fruit of the Mystery: ***Openness to the Holy Spirit***

Second Luminous Mystery: The Wedding at Cana

His mother said to the servants, "Do whatever He tells you."… Jesus said to them, "Fill the jars with water." And they filled them up to the brim.

(*John* 2:5-7)

One *Our Father*, Ten *Hail Marys*,
One *Glory Be*, etc.

Fruit of the Mystery: ***To Jesus through Mary***

Third Luminous Mystery: The Proclamation of the Kingdom of God

"And preach as you go, saying, 'The kingdom of heaven is at hand.' Heal the sick, raise the dead, cleanse lepers, cast out demons. You received without pay, give without pay." (*Matthew* 10:7-8)

One *Our Father*, Ten *Hail Marys*,
One *Glory Be*, etc.

Fruit of the Mystery: ***Repentance and Trust in God***

Fourth Luminous Mystery: The Transfiguration

And as He was praying, the appearance of His countenance was altered and His raiment become dazzling white. And a voice came out of the cloud saying, "This is My Son, My chosen; listen to Him!

(*Luke* 9:29, 35)

One *Our Father*, Ten *Hail Marys*,
One *Glory Be*, etc.

Fruit of the Mystery: ***Desire for Holiness***

Fifth Luminous Mystery: The Institution of the Eucharist

And He took bread, and when He had given thanks He broke it and gave it to them, saying, "This is My body which is given for you."… And likewise the cup after supper, saying, "This cup which is poured out for you is the new covenant in My blood."

(*Luke* 22:19-20)

One *Our Father*, Ten *Hail Marys*,
One *Glory Be*, etc.

Fruit of the Mystery: ***Adoration***

First Sorrowful Mystery: The Agony in the Garden

In His anguish He prayed with all the greater intensity, and His sweat became like drops of blood falling to the ground. Then He rose from prayer and came to His disciples, only to find them asleep, exhausted with grief. (*Luke* 22:44-45)

One *Our Father*, Ten *Hail Marys*,
One *Glory Be*, etc.

Fruit of the Mystery: ***Sorrow for Sin***

Second Sorrowful Mystery: The Scourging at the Pillar

Pilate's next move was to take Jesus and have Him scourged. (*John* 19:1)

One *Our Father*, Ten *Hail Marys*,
One *Glory Be*, etc.

Fruit of the Mystery: ***Purity***

Third Sorrowful Mystery: The Crowning with Thorns

They stripped off His clothes and wrapped Him in a scarlet military cloak. Weaving a crown out of thorns they fixed it on His head, and stuck a reed in His right hand… (*Matthew* 27:28-29)

One *Our Father*, Ten *Hail Marys*,
One *Glory Be*, etc.

Fruit of the Mystery: ***Courage***

Fourth Sorrowful Mystery: The Carrying of the Cross

… carrying the cross by Himself, He went out to what is called the Place of the Skull (in Hebrew, Golgotha). (*John* 19:17)

One *Our Father*, Ten *Hail Marys*,
One *Glory Be*, etc.

Fruit of the Mystery: ***Patience***

Fifth Sorrowful Mystery: The Crucifixion

Jesus uttered a loud cry and said, "Father, into Your hands I commend My spirit." After He said this, He expired. (*Luke* 23:46)

One *Our Father*, Ten *Hail Marys*,
One *Glory Be*, etc.

Fruit of the Mystery: ***Perseverance***

First Glorious Mystery: The Resurrection

You need not be amazed! You are looking for Jesus of Nazareth, the one who was crucified. He has been raised up; He is not here. See the place where they laid Him." (*Mark* 16:6)

One *Our Father*, Ten *Hail Marys*,
One *Glory Be*, etc.

Fruit of the Mystery: ***Faith***

Second Glorious Mystery: The Ascension

Then, after speaking to them, the Lord Jesus was taken up into Heaven and took His seat at God's right hand. (*Mark* 16:19)

One *Our Father*, Ten *Hail Marys*,
One *Glory Be*, etc.

Fruit of the Mystery: ***Hope***

Third Glorious Mystery: The Descent of the Holy Spirit

All were filled with the Holy Spirit. They began to express themselves in foreign tongues and make bold proclamation as the Spirit prompted them. (*Acts* 2:4)

One *Our Father*, Ten *Hail Marys*,
One *Glory Be*, etc.

Fruit of the Mystery: ***Love of God***

Fourth Glorious Mystery: The Assumption

You are the glory of Jerusalem... you are the splendid boast of our people... God is pleased with what you have wrought. May you be blessed by the Lord Almighty forever and ever.

(*Judith* 15:9-10)

One *Our Father*, Ten *Hail Marys*,
One *Glory Be*, etc.

Fruit of the Mystery: ***Grace of a Happy Death***

Fifth Glorious Mystery: The Coronation

A great sign appeared in the sky, a woman clothed with the sun, with the moon under her feet, and on her head a crown of twelve stars. (*Revelation* 12:1)

One *Our Father*, Ten *Hail Marys*,
One *Glory Be*, etc.

Fruit of the Mystery: ***Trust in Mary's Intercession***

This book is part of a non-profit mission.
Our Lord has requested that we
spread these words internationally.

Please help us.

If you would like to assist us financially,
please send your tax-deductible contribution
to the address below:

Direction for Our Times
9000 West 81st Street
Justice, Illinois 60458

708-496-9300
contactus@directionforourtimes.com

www.directionforourtimes.org

Direction for Our Times Ireland
Drumacarrow
Bailieborough
Co. Cavan
Republic of Ireland

+353 (0)42 969 4947 or +353 (0)42 969 4734
contactus@dfot.ie

Direction for Our Times is a 501(c)(3)
non-profit corporation. Contributions are
deductible to the extent provided by law.

The Volumes

Direction for Our Times
as given to Anne, a lay apostle

Volume One:	***Thoughts on Spirituality***
Volume Two:	***Conversations with the Eucharistic Heart of Jesus***
Volume Three:	***God the Father Speaks to His Children*** ***The Blessed Mother Speaks to Her Bishops and Priests***
Volume Four:	***Jesus the King*** ***Heaven Speaks to Priests*** ***Jesus Speaks to Sinners***
Volume Six:	***Heaven Speaks to Families***
Volume Seven:	***Greetings from Heaven***
Volume Nine:	***Angels***
Volume Ten:	***Jesus Speaks to His Apostles***

Volumes Five and Eight will be printed at a later date.

The Volumes are now available in PDF format for free download and printing from our website: www.directionforourtimes.org. We encourage everyone to print and distribute them.

The Volumes are also available at your local bookstore.

The "Heaven Speaks" Booklets

Direction for Our Times
as given to Anne, a lay apostle

The following booklets are available individually from Direction for Our Times:

Heaven Speaks About Abortion
Heaven Speaks About Addictions
Heaven Speaks to Victims of Clerical Abuse
Heaven Speaks to Consecrated Souls
Heaven Speaks About Depression
Heaven Speaks About Divorce
Heaven Speaks to Prisoners
Heaven Speaks to Soldiers
Heaven Speaks About Stress
Heaven Speaks to Young Adults

Heaven Speaks to Those Away from the Church
Heaven Speaks to Those Considering Suicide
Heaven Speaks to Those Who Do Not Know Jesus
Heaven Speaks to Those Who Are Dying
Heaven Speaks to Those Who Experience Tragedy
Heaven Speaks to Those Who Fear Purgatory
Heaven Speaks to Those Who Have Rejected God
Heaven Speaks to Those Who Struggle to Forgive
Heaven Speaks to Those Who Suffer from Financial Need
Heaven Speaks to Parents Who Worry About Their Children's Salvation

All twenty of the "Heaven Speaks" booklets are now available in PDF format for free download and printing from our website www.directionforourtimes.org. We encourage everyone to print and distribute these booklets.

Other books by Anne, a lay apostle

Climbing the Mountain
Discovering your path to holiness
Anne's experiences of Heaven

The Mist of Mercy
Spiritual Warfare
Anne's experiences of Purgatory

Serving In Clarity
A Guide for Lay Apostles
of Jesus Christ the Returning King

In Defense of Obedience
and
Reflections on the Priesthood
Two Essays on topics close to the Heart of Jesus

Interviews with Anne, a lay apostle

VHS tapes and DVDs featuring Anne, a lay apostle have been produced by Focus Worldwide Network and can be purchased by visiting our website at **www.directionforourtimes.org**

Jesus gives Anne a message for the
world on the first of each month.
To receive the Monthly Message you
may access our website at
www.directionforourtimes.org
or call us at 708-496-9300
to be placed on our mailing list.